SWEET CAROLINA

DEBBIE WHITE

ACKNOWLEDGMENTS

COVER DESIGN BY DANA LAMOTHE FROM DESIGNS
BY DANA

http://www.facebook.com/designsbydanaı

Editing by Daniela Prima from Prima Editing &
Proofreading Services
http://www.primaeditingproofreading.weebly.com/

CHAPTER ONE

J ack carried the baby car seat carrier by the handle, holding Ashton with a tight grip while the nurse wheeled Annie out to the car. Annie watched as Jack carefully snapped the car seat in place. With half of his body in and the other half out of the car, Annie had a great view of his backside. She widened her eyes as she heard some grunting noises coming from inside the car. "Everything all right in there, Jack?"

"I'm making sure this car seat is secured," he said through gritted teeth.

"Why don't you come out and let me take a look?"

Jack slowly pulled back, and then not quite clearing the open car door, banged his head. "Ouch." He rubbed the top of his head.

Annie looked over her shoulder at the nurse, and then nodding, rose from the wheelchair. She took a few steps toward the car and peeked inside. "Looks good. I'll just slide in here next to the baby," she said, taking her place.

Jack waved goodbye to the nurse, and Annie flashed a broad smile. Once the nurse had turned away, Annie went to work fixing the car seat.

Jack hopped into the front seat and started the motor. He glanced back at Annie. "I knew it. I did something wrong," he said, palming the dashboard.

"No, you did a good job, really. It's just the one strap you missed. It can be tricky. We'll work on it together," she said, trying to soothe his ego.

Jack put the car in gear, checking his mirror three times before pulling out of the pickup zone. "Is the music too loud?" He peered at her from the rearview mirror.

"No, it's lovely. Jack, we aren't going to tiptoe around Ashton. We want him used to sounds." She chortled at his exaggerated attentiveness.

"I'm not used to having a baby around."

"I'm not either, but I think we'll be fine. I hope our families and friends will give us a few days before they come to visit."

"I told mine to wait until they were invited," Jack said boldly.

Annie twisted her mouth to the left and nodded. "I hope you didn't come across as angry."

"No, I just told them that my lovely wife, who just gave birth to my son, needs her rest."

Annie took in a deep breath. "Oh, I see," she said, turning her eyes to the view outside her window.

"I made sure the house is clean. I put clean sheets on the bed, all the laundry is folded and put away, and I even gave the dogs a bath," Jack said, interrupting her silent time.

"Oh, how very thoughtful of you, thanks. I need to get into a routine with breastfeeding and pumping and all of that."

"Don't you worry about a thing, Annie. I'm here to help." He looked at her again through the rearview mirror.

"Help? How are you going to help with breastfeeding?" she said, giggling again.

"I'll help by changing diapers, fetching things, warming up bottles—that sort of thing. I'm here for you," he said, sounding almost rehearsed.

"Okay, where is Jack and what have you done with him? And more importantly, which one has transformed you from the man I love to the man who will drive me crazy if he keeps up this talk? Grandmother or Auntie? Or wait—was it my sister, Mary?"

Jack hung his head low, and then quickly raised it again, staring at the road in front. "Grandmother," he said shyly.

"Well, don't listen to her. I'll be happy for your help, Jack. I really will, but let's not get crazy. We need a plan."

Annie began to tell Jack her solution, and he listened carefully on the drive home. Once inside, Annie sat on the couch and played with the dogs for a minute. "Let them sniff Ashton," she said to Jack.

Jack held the seat by the handle and lowered it to Buffy and Isla's level. Their noses wiggled and snorted, and their tails wagged a mile a minute. Before he could pull up the car seat, Buffy licked Ashton across the face, and Isla put her big paw on the side of the carrier.

"Whoa, dogs!" Jack said, yanking the carrier up. Baby Ashton stirred.

"Let's get him settled into his new cradle," Annie said, leading the way to Ashton's bedroom.

"I love the paint color; it's so ..."Jack stopped without finishing his sentence.

"Boyish?" Annie suggested, finishing his sentence.

The room had been painted blue. Keeping with the jungle theme they'd chosen, there was also a large mural on one wall depicting a tree and animals that seemed to come to life, matching his comforter and bumper pad in the crib. Jack carefully lifted Ashton out of the carrier and gently lay him into the new cradle.

Annie got a kick out of how controlled and perceptive Jack became in the mission of lifting Ashton out of the carrier. His tongue slipped out of his mouth as he concentrated on his every move. He even grunted a little as he lifted the little guy out.

"He won't break, Jack," Annie said as she watched this very robot-like behavior from Jack.

Except for one sudden moment when Ashton's hands flew up to the face, he fell back asleep, and Jack and Annie quietly tiptoed out of the room.

"I thought we weren't going to tiptoe," Jack whispered.

Annie shrugged her shoulders and poked out her bottom lip. "I changed my mind."

Jack put his arm around her and pulled her close. "And anytime my baby wants to change her mind, that's okay with me." He nuzzled her ear with his mouth.

"Okay, where's my phone? I'm calling Grandmother!"

❧

LIKE MOST NEW PARENTS, JACK AND ANNIE HAD MANY

sleepless nights. Going on as little as three hours of sleep, Annie found the comfy rocking chair in Ashton's nursery a suitable replacement for her bed. Not really, but when you were holding a bundle of joy like Ashton, all reasonable expectations flew out the window.

Jack poked his head inside Ashton's room. "Good morning," he said, his eyes immediately moving to Ashton.

"Good morning. Another rough night," she said as she rocked him.

"He was doing so well, too," Jack said, stepping inside the space and crossing toward them both.

"I know. He's drinking more ounces. I do believe he's having a growth spurt."

Jack nodded. "He's our growing boy." He slid his hand up and down the baby's torso.

"Can you hold him? I have to go to the bathroom," she said, standing up and handing over Ashton.

Jack began to rock him in his arms while Annie dashed to the bathroom. While Annie finished up, she could hear Jack singing to Ashton. She turned the water off, straining her ears so she could hear clearer. A wide smile crossed her face as she listened to some made-up song Jack sang and his substituted hums when he couldn't think of a word quickly enough.

Annie back stepped into the room and held out her arms. "Okay, thanks. I can take over now."

"No, why don't you go get a cup of coffee, a glass of juice, take a shower, or do something for yourself? I have this," he said, repositioning Ashton in his arms.

"You don't have to ask me twice," she said, leaning over and kissing Ashton on the cheek then turning her warm kisses to Jack. "Love you both," she said, moving backward.

Annie quickly made her way to the kitchen, where she made herself a cup of coffee. It'd been the first time in a while since she'd enjoyed a hot cup of coffee without either a big belly or holding a baby. She limited how much caffeine she drank, anyway, due to the breast-feeding. She didn't realize how much she missed the taste of a good cup of coffee.

After her coffee, she took a fifteen-minute shower. She must have let the water run over her face and down her body a good five minutes. She washed her hair not just once, but twice, and she even let the cream rinse stay on a little longer. She took her time combing out her hair, and then she put on a pair of real pants and a shirt, not just a clean nightgown and housecoat. She even spritzed on some cologne and dabbed a little lipstick on. She actually felt human for the first time in about three weeks.

She peered into Ashton's room. Jack had rocked the baby to sleep in the wooden chair, and apparently, had rocked himself right to sleep as well. A soft but steady snore escaped his lips. She quietly walked over and leaned down, tapping him once before taking Ashton out of his arms.

His eyes immediately opened. "Huh, what?" he said a bit confused.

"It's just me. Thanks for looking out for him. I feel like a new person," she said, taking the baby and placing him in his cradle. "Come on," she said, reaching her hand out to Jack.

Jack rose from the chair and held her hand. Annie squeezed his hand as they crept out of the room. Once out in the hallway, Annie let go of his hand and hugged him.

"What's that for?"

"I love you so much. We're going to get through this. One more week and he'll be a month old. I think it'll be the turning point for us."

"Let's take advantage of him sleeping. I have some-thing I want to show you."

Annie took a few steps away from the room and then stopped.

"What's wrong?"

"I don't really know. I feel a bit of anxiety," Annie said, knitting her brows together.

"You've been spending way too much time in there and with him. You have to let me help more."

Annie nodded. "I know, but it's just so hard to give up my motherhood right now."

"You're not giving up your motherhood, Annie. You'd never give that up. You're letting me ... hello ... the daddy, help more." Jack lowered his head so he could focus on her eyes.

"Okay, I'll try. What is it you that you wanted to show me?"

Jack showed her the diagram for the layout for his new shop. His dad had given him one of the garages they owned. It was in a perfect location, was gated for security, and the best part, there would be no rent to pay —a deal too good to pass up.

Annie tried to focus on the schematic, but her mind kept floating to the nursery.

"Did you hear that?" she said suddenly.

Jack cocked his head to listen. "No, what did you hear?"

"I thought I heard Ashton cry."

"Annie, if he cried, we'd hear him. The nursery is just down the hall."

They'd made a conscious decision to use the extra

room down the hall on the first floor as the nursery. Neither of them was ready to move Ashton to one of the kid rooms located upstairs. "He's so little. I want him closer to us," she recalled saying.

Jack sighed. "I think you need to talk to someone, Annie. I don't know if this is normal. You can't even walk away a little from his room without panicking."

Annie averted her eyes from him, and instead, looked at the table and began to fiddle with the corner of his diagram. "I'll be all right. Just give me a little more time. He's so little and precious. I can't bear to be too far from him."

Jack pulled her into his arms and hugged her tightly. Annie could feel his concern through his touch. Tears began to form. She quickly swept them away, staring off into space.

MILLY HAD AGREED TO WATCH ASHTON. SHE'D TAKEN care of Crystal, Richard and Diane's little girl, until she'd started pre-kindergarten, and she still provided after school care for her. Annie's only concern now was if Milly could handle taking care of a baby, since it had been a while.

"Now, everything you need is in the diaper bag," Annie said, pulling things out one by one.

"Yes, dear, we've been over this a few times. And I have your cell number programmed as well as 9-1-1."

"I'm sorry, Milly. It's just my first day back to work, and I'm feeling a bit ..."

Milly wrapped her arms around Annie. "I get it. You're feeling a bit blue. But think about all the moms who have to take their children to strangers. Little Ashton gets to stay with Nana," she said, gazing over at Ashton.

Ashton kicked a few times, causing the toys attached to his carrier to move and make noise. Then he kicked some more after he realized he was the one making the movement. A small giggle escaped his mouth.

"Look, he's smiling. He's happy about being here with Nana." Milly reached down and tugged at his foot.

"Okay, I'm leaving now," Annie said, leaning down to kiss Ashton on the cheek.

"Have a great day," Milly said, walking her to the front door.

"I'll try. I'm only working until two o'clock. I should be here by two thirty."

"If you have any errands to run, do them. We'll be right here waiting for you," Milly said, reaching down and lifting Ashton out of his carrier.

Annie tipped her head. "Bye," she said, waving goodbye.

Annie got in her car and drove to the bakery. Her thoughts kept flipping back to Milly and all the things she'd packed in the diaper bag. "Diapers, check. Bottles, check. Pacifier, check. Extra clothes, check." Annie sighed. She pulled into the parking lot and soon entered her shop. She flipped on the lights and began heating up the ovens, gathering supplies, and filling the register with funds from the safe. Before long, she was joined by Betsy.

"Annie!" Betsy hugged her strongly and then stepped back. "It's so good to see you." A smile crossed her face.

"It's good to be back ... I think," Annie said quietly.

"He's in great hands, Annie. Listen, why don't you help me in the kitchen?" Betsy took off around the counter, tossing her purse behind the cabinet door and grabbing her apron off the hook. Annie followed her.

Betsy picked up the clipboard and flipped the pages. "Today, we're making holiday cupcakes. Can you believe it's October already?" Betsy crossed over to the large metal shelves and began pulling bags of sugar, flour, and other ingredients.

Annie watched on. "Jack's birthday is at the end of this month," Annie said, shaking her head.

"Are you going to throw him a party?"

"I don't know, I really haven't had a chance to think about it," Annie said, lifting the mixer heads and popping in the beaters.

"It's my favorite time of the year. Fall." Betsy smiled.

"Mine, too. Well, I also love spring. And I love summer, but only when we're in *Lady Powell*, or visiting the beach."

"Or sitting under that gorgeous magnolia tree," Betsy said, nodding.

"Yes, that, too." Annie walked around the counter and gazed at the recipes Betsy would be preparing. "Pumpkin Swirl, one of the customers' favorites."

"Everything pumpkin," they both said at the same time, and then laughed loudly.

"You know, I think I will have a little party for Jack. He's been working so hard, and he's been such a help with Ashton. He deserves recognition on his special day."

"There you go. I can make a cake," Betsy said, looking up.

"I haven't planned a real party since ..."Annie said, trailing off.

"Your housewarming, September last year."

"He loves Halloween parties, and since his birthday is on the thirty-first, why not?"

"Sounds great. He'll love it. And Halloween is on a Saturday this year, so it's a perfect time for a party."

Annie began to dump the flour and sugar mixture in the large stainless steel bowls. "By the way, how are Grandmother and Auntie? I've meant to visit, but I've been so exhausted."

"They're doing okay, but since Mary moved out, I see them becoming a bit more reclusive, a bit down in the dumps."

"Really? Do you think it's time for them to move to the cottage?"

"Well ..." Betsy stopped and locked eyes with Annie. "Charles and I had an idea. We wanted to discuss it with you, but since you brought them up ..."

Annie rocked back on her heels. "Okay, go ahead."

"What do you think about Charles and me moving in with them?"

CHAPTER TWO

A nnie had to hand it to Betsy and Charles. They'd come up with a better solution than any of them had. Grandmother and Auntie had grown to love them and enjoyed their company. Betsy and Charles both had experience in caring for the elderly, and the patience of a saint, to boot. If Grandmother and Auntie were on board with this idea, then Mary and Annie both agreed they'd give them their blessings.

Annie made arrangements to meet Mary over at Grandmother and Auntie's house. Charles and Betsy would already be there. While Annie waited for Mary, she sat in her car and pulled up pictures of Ashton on her phone. She hated to admit her lack of knowledge when it came to anything electronic. But when your camera is part of your phone, you didn't have to be a pro. She touched his round cheeks with her fingers and smiled. Just then, Mary pulled up behind her. Annie put her phone away and stepped out of the vehicle.

She pulled her lightweight coat together and lifted the collar. She crossed her arms and hugged them. "Brr, it's getting cold," she said.

"I think we may get hit with an early winter," Mary said, walking over to her.

"Ready?" Annie said, nodding toward the house.

"Ready as I'll ever be," she said, taking the first step.

"Well, dears, it's so nice of you two to visit. Tea?" Lilly said with a raised brow.

Annie nodded and then turned to Mary and smiled. She turned her attention back to Grandmother. "Yes, that would be nice."

Lilly followed Betsy into the kitchen, where they could hear them chatter away while they prepared the tea. Annie and Mary sat down on the couch and smiled at Charles. "Grandmother seems like she's in a great mood. This might go over better than I thought. Where's Auntie?"

"She'll be out soon. She is changing her blouse. She spilled something on it."

Annie tipped her head. She knew all too well that both her grandmother and auntie always dressed appropriately, and most of the time overdressed. Annie sniggered. "They're too funny. We're family. No need to dress up."

"Well, you know your grandmother and auntie," Charles said with a twinkle in his eyes.

Mary crossed her legs and began to pump her foot. Finally, Annie placed her hand on Mary's knee to get her to stop. Mary then uncrossed her legs at the knees and crossed them at the ankles. Soon her foot began twitching back and forth. Annie sighed.

"Let me see if I can help them." Annie rose from the coach and made her way to the kitchen. Just then, the ladies came out holding trays with cups, a small ceramic pot, and a plate of butter cookies. Annie reached for the one Grandmother held. "Let me help you."

Annie walked behind the two ladies, and soon Auntie joined them with a freshly laundered blouse.

"Hello, Mary. Hello, Annie," she said in her bubbly voice.

"Good day, Auntie," Mary said.

Annie smiled at her. "It's nice to see you. I have pictures of Ashton to share," she said, retrieving her phone to show them. They took a few minutes to look at the pictures and then Annie sat back down next to Mary.

Charles cleared his throat. "Are you and Danny all settled into your new place, Mary?"

"Yes, we're very comfy."

"And you and Jack are working things out being new parents?" he asked, changing his focus from Mary to Annie.

Annie nodded. "Yes, it took us a little while, but I do believe we now have a routine. And we're so blessed to have Jack's mother, Milly, watching him so I can go back to work."

"She's a doll for helping," Auntie said, bringing the teacup to her lips She quickly reached for a napkin to catch the dribble making its way down her chin. She let out a small giggle.

"How would you like to have Charles and Betsy be your roommates?" Mary said, blurting out the plan without so much of a hint it was coming.

"Well, what I think Mary is asking," Annie began, cutting a look toward Mary, "is if you'd like to have their company all the time. Now that Mary has moved out, you have an extra room." Annie twisted her neck, and then hid her mouth with the palm of her hand so no one could see as she stuck her tongue out at her sister.

Lilly snorted, and Patty breathed out the breath she'd apparently been holding and gasped. "Share a room ... here?"

Annie's eyes widened when she realized what they were getting at. Charles and Betsy were not married. They didn't care what folks did outside of their house, but there was no way in heaven or earth they'd let that go on under their roof. "Oh, that's right. That might present a problem." She looked over at Charles and then Betsy for help.

"Problem solved, Lilly. We'd never think of disrespecting you or your rules. In fact, we're a bit old-school, too." Charles reached over and picked up Betsy's hand and showed them the thin gold band on her finger. "We got married yesterday."

Annie's jaw dropped, Mary gasped, and more loud sighs came from Lilly and Patty.

"Congratulations, you two!" Annie leaped from the couch and ran to them, hugging them both. "This is great news," she said, looking over her shoulder at Mary.

Mary nodded. "Yes it is, isn't it Grandmother and Auntie?"

"Well, I wish you had let us in on the little secret. We would have loved to do something special for you." Lilly lifted her chin and grunted.

"We've both been married before, so a simple ceremony was all that we wanted," Betsy said, squeezing Charles's hand.

"But no decision has to be made today. Think it over," Charles said, speaking up.

"That's right. We're just tossing the idea out there. With Mary living across town, and me and Jack out on the island, we'd feel better about them living here. But it's up to you, the decision is yours and yours alone to make." Annie wondered if the reverse psychology was working.

As they all took in Charles and Betsy's exciting news, they finished sipping their tea and enjoying the cookies. They talked about family stuff, Jack's new business adventure, and of course, Ashton. After about ninety minutes, the visit came to an end. Grandmother, Auntie, Charles, and Betsy walked Mary and Annie to the front door.

"Does this mean that Betsy won't be working at the bakery anymore?" Patty asked.

Annie stopped in her tracks and whirled around. "Betsy, I'll let you answer that."

"I'll still work there, but I'd like to cut my hours. Annie is looking for a new baker now."

Annie tipped her head. "Yes, and it is proving to be more difficult than I'd hoped."

"You know, we could clear out the attic, and it would be a great mini apartment," Lilly said out of the blue.

Annie had forgotten about the space. It held boxes,

stacked to the ceiling, an old brass bed, and who knows what else. A private bath adjoined the area, and a small landing near the staircase gave it a nice private feel.

"Grandmother, that's a great idea. It really is a nice space. We used to play up there a lot when we were kids."

"We could have a weekend where we all pitch in to clean it up, get it painted, etcetera," Mary said, reaching her arm out to stroke Lilly's arm.

"So, does this mean we're moving in?" Charles said, followed by a burst of laughter.

"I think so," Patty said, nodding toward her sister, Lilly.

"Grandmother, that's so kind of you to offer them the attic space. It really will make a nice apartment, and you'll have them right here with you. I may be losing the best baker for Sweet Indulgence, but you'll be gaining a great cook, baker, and the companionship of two very special people." Annie smiled over at the newlyweds.

"Just tell us when and we'll bring the reinforcements," Mary quipped.

"Sounds like a plan," Betsy said, walking them to the door.

"See you tomorrow, Betsy," Annie said, walking out the front door.

"Peter will be there tomorrow," Betsy said, bobbing

her head between bodies to make eye contact with Annie.

"Is he fully trained? He can do everything you can do?"

"He still has a few things to learn, but he's catching on fast. I'll be there to help guide him, but he might be the next baker, and no need to look any further."

Annie tilted her head and pursed her lips tightly. "That would be the answer to all my prayers."

Mary leaned in and kissed her grandmother and auntie on the cheek and then Annie did the same. The two women walked down the sidewalk together, very happy with how things went.

Annie stood at her car, with one hand on the passenger door. She quickly opened the door and tossed her purse on the seat. "It couldn't have gone any better." She slammed the door shut.

"I know you probably didn't like the way I handled it, but I didn't see any reason to pussyfoot around the issues. We'd still be trying to discuss it if I hadn't just jumped in and blurted out the reason we were there."

"I get it. I try to handle them with kid gloves, but they can deal with almost anything. Their age is just a number. They've seen a lot and have been around the block a few times. They're very intelligent women. They know this is the aging process. No matter how much we hate it and don't want to admit it, it is what it is, and when family offers help and solutions, you just need to give in some."

"I couldn't agree more. And what about those two lovebirds?"

"I know, I think that was a last-minute decision on their part, but it's all good. I'm happy for them, and I think it really sealed the deal." Annie walked around the back of her car. "Have a great day, sis." She crossed to the driver's side and opened the door, about to slide in.

"Hey, Annie?"

Annie rose up and made eye contact with Mary. "Yes?"

"If Danny and I did what Charles and Betsy did, would you be as understanding?"

Annie placed a hand on her car roof. Knitting her brows together, she let out a long sigh. "If that's what you two choose to do, then I guess we'd have to accept it. I would much rather give you a real wedding. Mom and dad would have liked to see you have the wedding of your dreams. There's money in the trust for that, too."

"I know, but Danny and I aren't the church type."

"Doesn't have to be in a church. Jack and I got married under that big, old sweet magnolia tree," she said, recalling their beautiful day.

"We don't have anything like that, but we're still thinking about it."

"Are you officially engaged? Where was I when you made this announcement?"

"No, not officially. We don't do anything the conventional way."

"That's true," Annie said, giggling.

"Well, hug that nephew of mine. I'm coming over soon for my auntie fix. That, and to see that big puppy, Isla."

"She's growing as fast as Ashton. Yes, please come by. Bring Danny, too. No need to call, just drop by. Oh, and don't forget Jack's birthday bash, two weeks from tomorrow."

"Oh, that's right. We'll be there." Mary blew Annie a kiss.

Annie reciprocated and then got into her vehicle and drove off.

CHAPTER THREE

T alk about anxiety. Annie had plenty to go around, and it didn't just involve her reluctance to be too far away from Ashton. Throwing Jack a birthday party proved to be a bit more challenging than maybe Annie bargained for. But like anything, she took the task at hand by the horns, and made it the best she could. And from the sounds of it, she did a pretty good job.

"Annie, what you've done for Jack is so nice. I love the carved jack-o'-lanterns all over the place," her best friend and one of the original sorority sisters, Vicky said.

"And where in the world did you find the little pumpkin lights?" Mary asked.

"Craft store in town," Annie said, admiring the stringed lights.

"Well, everything is very nice," Vicky said, wrapping her arm around Annie.

"Please enjoy yourselves. There's plenty of food and drink. I'm going to go rescue the birthday boy from Grandmother," Annie said, stepping away from the huddle.

Ashton bobbled his toys while he sat on Jack's lap. He put everything in his mouth, so Annie and Jack made sure all his toys were of the finest materials. In fact, Jack made a teething toy for him out of solid maple, sanded smooth with no chemicals or stains. Ashton gummed it to death and had it in his mouth now.

Annie held out her arms. "Come to Mommy."

Jack leaned in and kissed both Ashton and Annie on the cheek. "I'm going to go over and talk with Major Scott Collins." His voice boomed when he said the man's name.

Annie chuckled. "Yes, why don't you." She sat down next to her grandmother while she bounced Ashton on her knee. She watched as Jack made his way over to Scott. He always mock saluted him before engaging in conversation with him. Annie wondered if Jack missed his opportunity to join the military. She drew in a deep breath and let it out slowly; the selfish side of her was glad he'd never been. Annie's awareness of some stuff regarding Danny and his PTSD that Mary was dealing with, gave her a window into what could happen to the men and women who serve, especially during conflict. Knowing how inevitable war could be, Annie, now the mother of a son, held her baby even closer.

Soon all the ladies gathered around Annie and her grandmother, Ashton drawing them in like a magnet. Everyone wanted to hold him. He got passed around like the football during their family-friendly Thanksgiving football game.

Annie had made costumes optional, and most people came dressed in street clothes, but it turned out many wanted to get into the spirit of Halloween. Mary and Danny came dressed as Bonnie and Clyde, and Annie had found a cute clown sleeper for Ashton and put some red lipstick on his cheeks. Grandmother and Auntie wore dark clothes and white crocheted shawls wrapped around their shoulders. They wore large hats secured under their chin with wide ribbon and told everyone they were dressed up as pioneer women. Annie laughed but then realized it wasn't too far from the truth. Those two really were pioneer women!

The children played games like bobbing for apples, fishing for toys out of a large plastic wading pool, and carving pumpkins.

"I think I'm going to go over and see the young people play some games," Patty said.

Annie tipped her head.

"Wait for me, I'll join you," Grandmother said, trailing behind her.

"Your grandmother and auntie are sure spry women for their age," Vicky said.

"Yes, they really are. I hope they'll always have good health." Annie drew in her bottom lip as her eyes welled up. "How's your house coming along?" she asked, changing the subject.

"It's coming along well. In fact, we should be moved in the week before Christmas."

"Wow, that's such a busy time."

"Yes, but it will be so nice to be in our dream home. I think we'll have a little get-together for New Year's Eve."

"That will be nice. By the way, have you heard from our wayward college sisters, Cassie and Jessica? I've invited them over twice since Ashton came home and they haven't come yet. The last time I saw them was at my baby shower."

Vicky shook her head. "No, I haven't. I've just talked to them on the phone a few times. They seem to be doing all right."

"Yeah, I've talked to them on the phone, too, but it sure would be nice to see them. I get it, though. They have their families, and I'm sure their time is stretched, just like mine."

Vicky drew in a deep breath and blinked a few times.

"I'm sorry. I didn't mean to ..."

"No worries. It's just something we have to get used to. We won't be having any children."

"Vicky, what about adoption?"

"We inquired, but they are discouraging us because Scott is in the military."

"That's just stupid. You two would make great parents, military or no military. What does that mean exactly, anyway?"

"We might get stationed somewhere else, I guess, before the process can be finalized."

"Well, get another attorney to give an assessment. I'm sure something can be done. They shouldn't be able to use the military as a reason for not granting the adoption. That's ... that's being prejudiced."

Vicky wiped the tears that rolled down her cheeks. "It does seem so wrong. We have so much love to give. We have a new beautiful house with four bedrooms, and we earn a decent income."

"Don't give up. Promise me you won't give up," Annie said, turning and placing both hands on Vicky's arms.

Vicky nodded. "Okay, we won't, I promise."

"And let's also make a pinky promise right now that we're going to go see those two college sisters of ours shortly. If they won't come to us, we'll go to them."

Broadening her smile to match her excitement, Vicky agreed. "Deal," she said, holding out her pinky.

∼

Annie flipped the light switch off and closed the door about halfway as she stepped out into the hallway.

"He's worn out," Jack whispered.

"It was all the excitement and being passed around to everyone. He will either sleep great, or he'll be over-stimulated and wake up a bunch of times."

"Think positive," Jack said, leading Annie down the hall toward their bedroom.

Sitting on the side of the bed, Annie rubbed lotion onto her feet and hands. Then she applied night cream to her face. "Scott and Vicky want a child so badly."

"Why don't they adopt," Jack said, climbing under the covers.

"They've tried. It seems that being in the military is not something favorable in the adoption agencies' eyes."

"That's crazy. They should be so happy to have a very patriotic American loving family, who has so much love to offer. They should be so lucky to find a better placement for an adoptee."

"I told her as much, and to not give up."

"What's on your agenda for tomorrow?" Jack asked, snuggling with Annie.

"Well, it's Sunday, and I'm officially off, but I thought maybe I'd drive into town and check in on the bakery. We're in full swing for the holidays, now."

"You need to take your days off, Annie. We've talked about this before. Why hire staff if you won't let them work without being micromanaged?"

"I'm not micromanaging. I'm just ..."

Jack pursed his mouth and knitted his brows.

"Okay. I'm micromanaging."

"So, I say we lounge around in our pajamas, while sipping hot chocolate and watching old movies." Jack pulled her over on top of him. Her hair hung down, tickling his face. He reached up and tucked it behind her ears.

Annie leaned down, finding his warm and very inviting mouth. They kissed passionately, both realizing it'd been a while. Having a baby could sometimes change the pattern of romance. He ran his hands up and down her back, holding her tightly while kissing her. She let out a soft moan as he rolled her off. She ran her hands up and down his arms as he stared at her hungrily. Just as he made his next move, Ashton wailed.

Annie bolted straight up. "Ashton!"

"Wait a second, let's see if he goes back to sleep," Jack said through labored breathing.

She dropped back down and gazed at Jack. He leaned over and resumed his kisses. Suddenly, she held up her hands against his chest. "I'm sorry. I just have to check on him."

Jack rolled over onto his back and stared at the ceiling. Annie climbed out of bed and dashed down the hallway. She peeked into the room. Ashton had fallen back to sleep. Annie smiled as she quietly walked back to their bedroom. Jack's hands rested behind his head on the pillow.

"Everything all right?" he said, making eye contact with Annie.

"Sound asleep, just like you said. I'm sorry," she said, climbing back onto the bed next to him. She snuggled under his arm.

Jack slid his arm around her and held her tightly. "We have to make sure we keep our romance alive, Annie. It's very important. I know it's an adjustment, and I'm willing to wait, but I have needs, too."

Annie turned her head and studied his face. She reached up and gently stroked his face. He turned toward her, his eyes almost begging for her. "No need to wait, Jack. I love you. You are my world. Without you, there'd be no Ashton. I'll always have time for you." She found his mouth and kissed him deeply, teasing him with her tongue.

He slid out his other arm and pulled her in. "I love you, Annie," he said, devouring her mouth.

∼

"MORE HOT CHOCOLATE IS COMING UP," ANNIE CALLED from the kitchen.

"Okay, hurry. The movie is about to start," he said.

Annie could hear Ashton babbling in the background. She fixed the hot cocoa, plated the gooey cinnamon rolls, and headed to the living room where the three of them would enjoy a lazy Sunday. Nothing could be more perfect. Annie laid the tray on the coffee table, and with both hands on her hips, smiled at her two guys cuddled on the couch. "Make room for Momma," she said, squeezing in.

Jack bounced Ashton in the air. He laughed as he came down into Jack's hands. The flames danced in the fireplace, and both Isla and Buffy lay tangled on their big fluffy bed, enjoying the warmth of the fire.

Annie brought the cup to her lips and blew on it. "This was a great idea," she said, smiling at the two of them.

"I do have a few good ideas now and then," he said, smiling back.

"And some good moves, too." She smiled when she recalled them together the night before.

Jack winked. He pounded his chest with the palm of his hand. "You Jane, me Tarzan."

Annie leaned forward and placed the cup on the table, picking up her phone. She turned toward Jack. "And in exactly three hours, when this little guy takes his nap, you can show me your Tarzan moves." She pulled in her bottom lip.

Jack patted her on the leg. "Now, that's what I'm talking about. The romance department is alive and well." He pulled her down and kissed her with Ashton right in the middle.

Ashton playfully waved his hands all around and reeled his head back and laughed. Soon Jack and Annie were laughing, too.

CHAPTER FOUR

Now that they were parents, Annie looked forward to her favorite season, fall, and all the holidays. Thanksgiving followed Halloween and then would come Christmas. It was also one of the busiest times of the year for the bakery.

Trying to remain the strong and independent businesswoman she'd become, Annie juggled motherhood, being a wife, as well as being the owner of Sweet Indulgence. Throw in the also being the oldest granddaughter and niece of two very needy elderly family members, and Annie could feel her once strong and independent self begin to crumble.

She stood at the kitchen sink, rinsing out Ashton's sippy cup, while Jack entertained him in the other room. The timer for their dinner went off, startling her. She dried her hands and opened the oven door. She drew in the smell of the baked pork chops and her mouth began to water. She put on a pair of oven mitts and pulled out the glass baking dish.

"Dinner is ready," she called out to Jack.

Jack came in carrying Ashton, swooping him up and down. He made airplane noises, and Ashton laughed and cackled as Jack flew him around the room. He flew Ashton right over to his high chair and buckled him in. Then he went over to help Annie. "Yum, something smells delicious," he said, coming up behind her.

"Just pork chops."

"Just pork chops," he said teasing. "They smell pretty darn good, for just being pork chops." He stuck his head around and kissed her on the cheek.

"Jack," she said, giggling.

"What?"

"Help me plate the food."

They sat down, and in between taking her bites, she fed Ashton.

"He seems to like the sweet potato," Jack said, observing Annie feeding him.

"He's five months old now; we can start experimenting with some different foods. I'd love to be able to make our baby food instead of buying the jarred stuff."

Jack forked a piece of his pork chop and brought it

toward his mouth. "Make his baby food? As if you have lots of spare time for that."

"I know, but I'd like to try. If we have to augment with jarred food, then that's what I'll do," she said, her voice catching.

Jack looked up. "Why are you crying, baby?"

"It's just that I'm trying to be everything for everyone, and not doing a very good job of it."

Jack slid his chair out and rested his hands on his lap. He tilted his head, while knitting his brows together. "Excuse me? You are more than everything to us. You are a perfect wife and mother, and that's all I care about."

"I have a business to run," she said, trying to hold back the tears.

"And you have help. You just need to let them do what you pay them to do."

Annie nodded. "It's hard to let go of something you've built from the bottom up."

"I get that, Annie, I do. But, if you want to see your business flourish, then you need to hire great people to help you, and then stand back and let them do it."

"And then there is everything with Grandmother and Auntie."

"What about them? If you're talking about the latest issue, that's been solved. Betsy and Charles have moved in."

"I know they have, but I can't help but think I've let Grandmother and Auntie down somehow, as well as my dad."

"Your dad would be proud of what you've accomplished, and I think he'd be happy with Betsy and Charles moving in over there. He wouldn't want you to give up your life entirely."

Annie hung her head down. Ashton squealed and began to kick the foot tray of his high chair. Annie returned her attention to him and smiled. "Want some more sweet taters?" She put a little on the edge of his baby spoon and slipped it between his lips. He kicked the foot tray again, and then in one quick movement, reached up and hit the spoon, knocking it out of Annie's hands.

"Whoa, big guy," Jack said, leaping out of his chair to help with the cleanup.

Annie took the bib Ashton wore and wiped the splattered potato off his face. She locked eyes with Jack and watched as he crossed the room and stood right in front of her. "What? Do I have sweet potato splatters on me too?"

Jack reached up and wiped the spot on her nose and then licked it. They both laughed, and soon Ashton laughed right along with them.

～

Jack wrapped his arms around her, and like a spoon, filled her spaces while holding on. She could feel his warm breath on her neck, and she snuggled deeper into his folds.

"I love you, Mrs. Powell," he said, whispering in her ear, lifting her hair a bit as he did with his breath.

She reached back and rubbed his arm. Since he'd started working with woodworking tools, he'd developed more muscles in his arms. "Ooh, I like what I feel," she teased.

"That right there, is pure muscle," he said, gloating.

She moved a few inches out of his reach and then turned over on her other side to now face him. She reached up and ran her fingers through his hair and down the side of his face. "I've been so preoccupied with my inadequacies that I've failed to ask you how your new business is going." She pulled herself toward him until she was just inches from his face. She stared into his deep eyes and waited for his response.

"First of all, you don't have any inadequacies. Stop with that kind of talk right now."

She tipped her head.

"It's going pretty good. I've gotten two new orders for Christmas yard decorations. One is for a set of reindeer and sled, and the other is for a cutout of Santa and Frosty."

"That's great, dear. This is the perfect time of year for that. What can I do to spread the word?"

"I've made some fliers for the bakery, and Dad put up one at the shop. Oh, and Diane is spreading the word at the vacation agency."

"Good," Annie said, nodding.

"I want to let people know that my skills are not just limited to Christmas decorations, but it's a start."

"Absolutely. We should take pictures of the cradle and the dining room table and everything else you've made."

"I'm way ahead of you. However, I do need your help with something." He reached out and pulled her even closer. He leaned over and kissed her softly on her mouth and then pulled back.

"What's that?"

"A name for the shop. We still need a name."

Annie's eyes widened. "I can't believe we forgot to name it!"

Jack brushed his hand down her head. "It's okay. We can do it now. Any ideas?"

Annie tilted her head and stared at the ceiling. A smile spread across her face. "I do. How about Powell's Sweet Wood Design?"

"That's perfect, Annie. I love it. I'll start on my sign tomorrow. I love how you thought of a way to incorporate sweet into the name."

"I'm glad I'm good for something," she said, winking.

"Oh, baby, you're good for a whole lot more," he said, kissing her.

No matter how tired Annie felt, when he kissed her, she suddenly felt like she was twenty years old and full of vigor. She kissed him back, trailing sweet kisses up and down his neck, finally resting her warm lips on his.

"I'M CALLING TO INVITE YOU ALL OVER TO THE HOUSE FOR Thanksgiving," Annie said to Milly on the phone.

"Are you sure?"

"I'm very sure. We'd love it if the grandparents could come, too. Grandmother and Auntie will be here. They love visiting with Cora and Polly. We'd also like to extend the invitation to Danny's folks, Susan and Preston." Annie waited for Milly to make an excuse for them.

"Okay, we'll come, and I'll let Susan know about your invite, but no promises there. They might have plans with that uppity social club they belong to. I don't understand how they can put that first before family."

Milly sighed. "You can be assured that the rest of us will be there, but you must let me help do some of the cooking, Annie."

"Jack is going to fry the turkey, so if you want to bring your homemade mac and cheese, that would be great. I'll ask Mary to bring a couple of pies and Grandmother and Auntie will make their cranberry sauce."

"I know my mother would love to make her dressing," Milly said.

"Okay, that sounds great. I'll make sweet potatoes. Ashton loves them. I might make a small batch of mashed potatoes, too. Come over early. Jack wants to toss the football around. The weather is supposed to be great. We can take a walk along the pathway that leads down to the beach. It'll be so much fun having you all here at Sweet Magnolia," Annie said, smiling through the phone.

It was a very special day, indeed, and the weatherman didn't disappoint them in the least. While the men tossed the football around, the women chattered and cooed over Ashton. After they ate a very hearty dinner, the group went for a walk. Jack pushed Ashton's stroller, and the men brought up the rear, while the women talked up front. After the brisk walk down to the beach, the group agreed they'd made room for some pumpkin and pecan pie.

After the last person left Sweet Magnolia, Annie dropped down on the sofa and placed her feet up on the coffee table. Buffy hurdled her little body up on the sofa and laid her head on Annie. "Another Powell-McPherson holiday celebration success." She patted Buffy's head and scratched her ears.

"Little Ashton is pooped. He went right to sleep," Jack said, sitting down. He patted her leg. "And, a great dinner, Annie." He leaned over and kissed her on the cheek.

"Thank you, sir. The turkey was delicious and so moist." She licked her lips, recalling the savory flavor of the turkey.

"We're really lucky, you know that?"

Annie nodded. "I have to pinch myself every now and again. We are."

"Tomorrow is Black Friday. Instead of going out in all the shopping hysteria, why don't we get our tree?" Jack said.

"That's a great idea. It will be little Ashton's first time to a tree farm."

Jack ran his hand up and down her arm, sending chills up and down her spine. Every time he touched her, he sent some signal that made her stomach tighten and her heart flutter.

"It will be his first of many things. I'm making him

something really special for Christmas," Jack said with his eyes twinkling.

Annie leaned in suddenly and kissed him.

"What was that for?"

"Can't a woman kiss her man?"

"She sure can," he said, grabbing her hand and helping her up from the couch, causing Buffy to slide off onto the opposite cushion. Annie looked over her shoulder at Buffy and Isla as he led her down the hallway.

As they passed Ashton's room, they couldn't help but stop and peer in. Jack quietly pushed open the door. Annie stretched her neck to see over Jack's shoulder and then bobbed her head to the right for a better view.

"Aw, he looks so peaceful," Annie said, pulling her arm out and wrapping it around Jack's waist.

"And happy. See that little smile on his face?" Jack beamed. "One of these days, he's going to be a big boy ... off to his first day of school, his first swimming lesson, his first—"

Annie put her finger to Jack's lips. "I don't want him to grow up too fast."

"I know, but it's inevitable, Annie."

"I know, but for now, let's just enjoy him as a baby." She reached up and hung her arms around his neck, pulling him down. Their lips met, and soon a passionate kiss began.

With his free hand, Jack pulled Ashton's door closed, mumbling something against her lips.

Annie put her finger up to her mouth and whispered, "Shh."

The two walked hand in hand toward their bedroom, and Annie wondered if it was possible to be any more in love or be any happier.

CHAPTER FIVE

Thanksgiving came, then Christmas. Jack's business boomed during the holidays, and no one could have been more pleased or surprised than Annie on Christmas morning. Little Ashton, now well on his way to being a big boy, bounced up and down when he saw the brightly colored wagon Jack helped him unwrap. With Ashton's name clearly painted on the side, this was a special wagon, indeed.

"After it warms up some, let's bundle him up and take him for a spin," Annie said, smiling as Jack pulled him around the living room, with both Buffy and Isla chasing them. The shrill sounds of the child's pleasure blended with the dogs' excited barks.

"I have something else." Jack handed Annie the

wagon handle. "I'll be right back." He dashed out of sight, leaving Annie wondering what he'd forgotten.

"What's your daddy up to, huh?" She leaned in and tickled Ashton on his tummy. Annie could hear some commotion going on out on the front porch, along with footsteps, grunting, and the sound of wood scraping against wood. She knitted her brows together. "Come here, baby boy," Annie said, lifting Ashton out of the wagon and carrying him to the sofa.

They'd just sat down when both Buffy and Isla hopped up to join them. Annie cocked her head and waggled her finger at them. "You know you two are not supposed to be up here."

Jack opened the front door and poked his head inside. "Okay, I'm ready."

Annie pulled the afghan down from the back of the sofa and wrapped it around them both. "What are you up to?" she asked Jack.

Jack held the door open for them. Annie stepped out onto the front porch. She gasped. "Jack, oh, my! They are lovely." She dashed toward the whitewashed rockers with big red bows, and plopping down in one, she began to rock back and forth.

Jack joined her and sat in the second one. "Do you like the color? Because I can stain them darker."

"I love them. Did you make these?"

Jack nodded.

"You are so talented, Jack. And to think it was all hidden behind a dark suit."

Jack rocked with his head leaning back against the frame. "Yeah, I liked driving and working for the family, but when I started building our house with my own hands, something happened. I didn't realize it myself how much I'd enjoy working with wood and tools." He gazed over at them.

"Well, I'm super impressed. And when you can work at something you love and make money at it, that's just icing, right?"

"Yep."

Annie shivered and pulled the blanket tighter around Ashton. "I think we better go inside. It hasn't warmed up enough for me or him," she said, nuzzling his little neck and making him laugh.

AFTER ALL THE HYPE OF THE HOLIDAYS, SPRING CAME, AND with it came warmer weather. After hiring a couple more workers, Annie cut her hours back a little more. Peter became the full-time baker, with Betsy only coming in once in a while. Morgan left the state to follow her dream of becoming a marine biologist, and Toby and Keith ... well were Toby and Keith.

Rebecca and Michael's new restaurant was the talk of the town, and during their last visit, Annie confided in Jack that she thought that maybe Rebecca could be pregnant.

"Did you see the glow? That's also known as the early stages of pregnancy," Annie said, trying to convince him.

"I don't know. It seems they'd want to wait. They've only been married a little over a year and opened up a new restaurant."

"Bet me a dollar," Annie said, teasing him.

"I'll bet you a boat ride," he said, raising his brows.

Annie knew what he was hinting at—a boat ride without Ashton.

It wasn't too long after that conversation that Rebecca confided in Annie what Annie had known all along. Annie didn't let on though. "Congratulations, Rebecca," she said, hugging her.

"I've had a little bit of morning sickness, but nothing too bad. I'm hoping to work right up until the birth."

"There's no reason you can't. And besides, you're married to a doctor. Everything should just be great."

"Well, you know what they say about doctors being

bad patients? Well, they're bad parents-to-be, too." They both laughed.

Annie loved to tease Jack, and she also loved to see him sweat, so when he arrived home after work she set him up good.

"I saw Rebecca today," she said, while chopping onions for dinner.

"And?" he said, bending his ear to hear that he'd won the bet.

"She's been a little sick lately."

Jack sat up straight and widened his eyes. "Sick? Sick as in the flu?"

"*Hmm*, no, I don't think so." She continued to chop and now began to hum some song.

"Okay, Annie, give it to me straight. Is she or isn't she?" He crossed his arms over his chest and tilted his head.

"Well, let's just say, it's lovely weather for a boat ride."

Jogging around her in a circle, he grabbed her around the waist. "You mean she isn't pregnant? You mean I won?"

"Whoa, wait just a minute. I didn't say anything about you being right."

Jack let go and stood back. "But you said boat ride. That was the bet. You said I'd bet you a dollar, and I said

I'd bet you a boat ride ... alone ... without the kid." He looked over his shoulder at Ashton playing with Cheerios on his high chair tray.

Annie pursed her lips tightly. "You are already tired of our baby?" she said with a raised brow.

"No, of course not. I just want to be alone with my other baby," he said, reaching for her again.

Annie play slapped his hands away. "Well, for the record, Rebecca is pregnant."

Jack gasped. "I don't get it. Then why would I win?"

"It just so happens, Jack Powell," she said moving closer, "that I want to go on that boat ride, too." She reached up and wrapped her arms around his neck and stared into his eyes.

"You got me," he said, moving in closer and meeting her lips with his.

Still holding on to his neck, she leaned back and smiled. "You can't outsmart me, Jack."

He pulled her in and whispered in her ear, causing the hair on her arms to stand. A deep stirring in the pit of her stomach lurched and pulled. She pulled her in bottom lip and coyly smiled at him. "Love you, Jack," she said before finding his warm mouth once again.

∼

"WHAT DO YOU MEAN YOU DON'T KNOW WHERE Grandmother or Auntie are? You live with them," Annie said into the phone.

"Charles and I went out to dinner and a movie. When we came home they were gone," Betsy said.

Annie's heart began to race when she thought of the possible situations these two women could get themselves into. Annie took in a deep breath and let it out slowly. "Well, I'll call the police right now and report them missing."

Before they hung up the phone, Betsy and Charles agreed to stay put, while Jack, Annie, and little Ashton went searching. First stop, was to the church.

"I don't know. It's worth checking here. I usually bring them here to visit the grave sites, but just maybe they got a wild hair ..."Annie said, trailing off as she slid out of the passenger side. She ducked back in before closing the door. "I'll be right back." She pushed the door with her hip, causing it to shut.

Annie made a beeline to her parents' graves. She paid special attention not to step anywhere but in between the markers. There were no signs of Grandmother or Auntie. While there, she took a moment to brush off each site, and vowed to be back soon with flowers.

She dropped down into the passenger seat. "Nope,

not there." She casually looked back at Ashton seated in his car seat, playing with toys.

"Where to next?"

Annie drummed her fingers on the dashboard. "Maybe the clubhouse at the golf club? Daddy used to bring them there often, and then after he passed away, they kept going out there. They made friends even though they don't golf. It's a long shot, but that's all I have right now."

Annie searched high and low inside the dimly lit bar area. Empty, except for one table of regulars, she ran her hand along the dark shiny mahogany bar top and asked the bartender if he'd seen them. Her hunch was right, he hadn't. She made her way toward the sunny garden-style restaurant that also had an extended outside eating area. She asked a few of the staff if they'd seen them, but she already knew the answer. She kicked a stone out of her way as she walked along the path that led her back to the car. Her head hanging low, she tried to think where in the heck those two could go and how could they get there? Annie picked her head up and smiled. Mary!

She jogged back to the car and dropped into the car, breathing heavily. "Mary. I have to call Mary. Maybe she knows." She punched in her number. "Mary do you have Grandmother and Auntie with you?"

"No, why would they be with me?"

"They're missing, that's why," Annie screamed.

"Missing? What do you mean missing?"

Annie told her the entire story. Afterwards, Mary said she and Danny would drive around, too.

"I know I'm never right about anything, but what about Black Eyed Pea?"

"Black Eyed Pea?" Annie knitted her brows together.

"It wouldn't hurt to check. We've checked everywhere else," Jack said, driving toward the restaurant.

Annie pulled herself out of the car and sighed. "I'll be back," she said, walking slowly toward the front of the restaurant. As she got closer, she could see two silver-haired women sitting in a booth near the window. Annie picked up her pace and tore into the restaurant, soon standing front and center of the booth. There, calmly sitting, were her grandmother and auntie, sipping on Bloody Marys and eating shrimp and grits. "Grandmother! Auntie!" Annie said, looking at one and then the other, glaring at them both as she did.

"Annie," Patty said.

"Annie? That's all you can say? We've been looking all over town for you. You scared us." She sat on the edge of the booth, sharing the seat with her grandmother.

Rebecca walked up to them and smiled. "Hey, Annie,

are you joining your grandmother and auntie for dinner?"

Annie widened her eyes. "No, I've lost my appetite."

Rebecca's jaw dropped. "That's not very nice to say."

Annie banged her hand on the table. "No, not because ... it's just because ..." She held her head in her hands and sobbed.

Rebecca, clearly confused by what was taking place, looked to Grandmother and Auntie for a clue.

"She's upset because we didn't tell anyone where we were going," Lilly said in a low tone as she patted Annie on the head. "Dear, please don't be so dramatic. We're out in public."

Annie's eyes popped wide open. "Dramatic? Don't be dramatic? I thought something bad had happened to my grandmother and auntie. My seventy-eight-year-old grandmother and auntie, I might add."

"Well, we don't have one foot in the grave, you know. Although, you'd like for us to feel that way. Having care-takers and time limits and bedtimes, too," Lilly said, scowling at Annie.

"Okay, you guys, quiet down. You're going to scare off my customers. This is a family thing. So, why don't you finish your dinner and drinks, while I talk to Annie," Rebecca said, pulling Annie up by the arm. She mouthed the words, "Follow me."

Annie hung her head low and followed Rebecca to the hostess station. "Listen, Annie, I know what they did is not right. You have to set some boundaries, I suppose. But, you know my grandmother is a little spitfire, too," Rebecca leaned in and whispered. "She's in the kitchen right now, telling them what to do." She pulled her head back and laughed.

Soon Annie laughed along with her. "I know, I get it. This has been such an ordeal. But they were totally on board with Charles and Betsy moving in. I don't know what happened."

"Well, ask them. If I know anything, I know they'll tell you the truth."

Annie nodded. "Thanks, Rebecca." She pulled her in for a hug.

"Listen, dinner and drinks are on the house. Now, scoot, and go get your house in order," she said, playfully swatting Annie on the rear.

Annie slowly made her way over to the table where she'd left them. Auntie slurped the rest of her cocktail. Pushing her glass aside, she sat back and sighed.

"Ready?" Annie asked, making a sweeping motion for them to exit the booth.

"What about our bill?" Lilly said as she scooted to the end of the bench.

"All taken care of." She opened her arms to them,

and with Grandmother on one side, and Auntie on the other, they walked out, holding their heads high, just as they'd always done, and how they always insisted Annie to do.

When Jack saw them coming, he shot out of the car and ran around to the passenger side car door and opened it.

"Hello, Jack," Patty said with a wide grin.

Jack's eyes darted from Annie to Lilly and then back to Auntie. "Howdy, Auntie Patty." He helped her take a seat.

Jack held out his hand to Grandmother. "Take my hand, Lilly." He walked her around to the other side and helped her slide in. Now, little Ashton had one of them on each side.

Annie lowered herself into the seat and buckled up. She leaned her head back on the headrest and sighed. Jack started the engine and drove. The only sounds came out of the back seat. Grandmother and Auntie played peekaboo, sang songs, and never once stopped making noise until they drove up to their house.

Jack cut the engine and looked over at Annie. "Want some help getting them inside?"

"I need to be in there for a bit. Why don't you go visit your folks for a while and come back for me in about an hour?"

Jack tipped his head. "Well, at least let me help you get them out of the car." He flew out, and before Annie could erase the fuzzy thoughts from her brain, he had them both waiting for her out on the sidewalk. She took them both by the hand, and soon they laced their hands in her arms. They made their way to the front stoop and entered the house. Charles and Betsy met them at the door.

"I'm so happy you found them," Betsy said.

"I don't know what all the fuss was about. We're perfectly able to go out and have dinner by ourselves."

Betsy began to reject that comment, but Annie held up her hand. Betsy backed away, allowing them to pass her.

"Can you please leave us alone for a moment?" Annie sat the two women down, and then went into the kitchen. "Tea or coffee?"

"Bloody Mary," they both called out.

Annie put her hands on her hips. She shook her head, and then mumbling to herself, "Why not?" proceeded to make not only them a Bloody Mary, but one for herself. She wasn't driving, after all.

"Okay, here are your drinks. Maybe now we can talk candidly." Annie sat down on the sofa across from them.

"Ooh, this is good, Annie. You make good Bloody Marys," Patty said, giggling.

Annie sighed. "Okay, the business at hand is not how well I make cocktails, but why you think you can just walk out of this house without so much as leaving a note."

"We did leave a note," Lilly said, puffing out her chest.

Annie raised her left brow. "Oh? And where is this note at?"

"We pinned it to the front door."

"The wind must have blown it off," Auntie Patty said, her eyes darting back and forth from Lilly to Annie. Then she slurped her drink.

"Okay, so at least you did do that. But in the future ... wait." Annie drew in a long drink through her straw, while she leaned back onto the sofa. She then moved forward and put her drink down on the table. "Okay, let's make a deal. If you want to go out, you leave a note, but you also call Mary and me to let us know. That way, if the note isn't found, we'll be able to tell Betsy and Charles. Agreed?"

Grandmother and Auntie nodded.

"Is there anything else we need to talk about?" Annie looked at them both for a reply.

"We want more freedom," Auntie blurted.

"Yes, we feel that although we do enjoy their company, we'd like to be able to do some things on our own, just like they do. They went off to dinner and a movie and left us here to twiddle our thumbs," Lilly said, twisting her shoulders back and forth and lifting her chin in the air.

"So were you jealous that they didn't include you? Don't you think they deserve any time alone?"

"Well, yes, I do think they deserve time alone, but so do we. We'd like to start going to the golf club again, maybe join the bridge club again, or go out to lunch once in a while with old ladies our age. We met Rebecca's grandmother tonight. She had us grabbing our sides, she's so funny," Patty said, laughing.

"Okay, so it seems that maybe you both have gotten your second wind in life. You want to get out and about. Are you both feeling well? No issues with mobility, right?"

"We get tired easily, we won't deny that. And we like to use someone's arm for security, and a cane now and then. But we're breathing, and our brain is still working, so yes, we want to get out more."

"I thought they were getting you out a lot. I'm sorry. When did that change?"

"They're good people, Annie. This is not about them doing anything wrong. And when we go to the plays with them, we always have a good time. But you can only go to plays so often."

"So, do you want to continue with this living arrangement with Betsy and Charles living here?"

Lilly looked over to Auntie and nodded. Auntie nodded back.

"Okay, so I'll let them know that this is more about you all wanting to get out more, and not about them," Annie said, standing.

"Yes, dear, that's exactly right."

"Maybe if they took you to more places, you'd be okay with that as well?" Annie said, hinting that maybe this was more about being left out and not really as much about their independence.

"Well, maybe," Lilly said.

"I'll be right back."

Annie walked up the stairs and rapped on Betsy and Charles's door. She'd not been up to the tiny apartment since they'd moved in. Betsy opened the door wide, a look of concern written all over her face. "Come in," she said, opening the door wider.

Annie stepped inside. She looked around the small space and smiled. "You really did a nice job with the apartment."

"I suppose now we have to move?" Betsy plopped down on the small sofa and cupped her face.

"No, no one is moving. This is the deal. They're feeling a bit left out. I understand you and Charles have a right to go out by yourself and I would never ask you not to. They're just feeling maybe a bit more house-bound, and to tell you the truth, they've gotten their second wind, and just want to enjoy life. So, I've agreed to allow them to catch a cab and go into town, as long as they let me, Mary, and you, all know. They said they left a note, but it must have blown off the front door. Also, they want to start playing bridge in the clubhouse. They both told me they wouldn't mind going out a bit more with you too, as well." Annie gathered in her lips and cocked her head.

"Okay, we'd love to take them out more, but when we were taking them out a lot, your grandmother started wheezing and coughing. We were worried it was too much. And Patty sometimes wanders off a bit, so we were worried she might be getting confused," Charles said.

Annie widened her eyes. "Well, the last time they went to the doctor, they got a pretty good bill of health. Grandmother is on medication for her heart, but Patty seemed fine. I'll make another appointment just to be sure, but I think everything is just fine. They're just not used to being told what to do and how to do it. I'm sure you can understand," Annie said, crossing her arms over her chest.

"Absolutely. We love your family and have tried our hardest to make them feel comfortable," Betsy said.

"Okay, so it's all settled. Things will be all right from now on." Annie held out her arms for a hug.

Betsy leaped up and ran into Annie's arms. "Thank you, Annie. I was so worried that things were going to change between us."

Annie pulled back from the embrace. "Are you kidding? You're a blessing to them, even if they don't realize it. And you're a blessing to us." She glanced at her watch. "Oh, Jack will be waiting for me outside with Ashton. I must run."

Annie took the stairs two at a time and when she landed, she rushed toward the living room. She popped her head inside and smiled. "Everything is good with Betsy and Charles. They love you two as well as we all do, and only want what is best for you. They understand your position and will see to it that you have many fun filled days. I must run now. Talk to you soon," she said, blowing them kisses.

"Tootles," Lilly called out.

"Adios," Patty said.

Annie stopped dead in her tracks and backed up a few steps, looking back into the living room. "Adios?"

"I'm learning Spanish from the gardener," Patty said, her eyes lighting up.

"Grandmother?" Annie said singingly as she headed toward the door.

"I'm on it, Granddaughter," Lilly called out.

~

ANNIE HOPPED INTO THE PASSENGER SEAT AND LET OUT A deep breath.

"Everything settled?" Jack asked.

"As settled as they can be. My grandmother and auntie are crazy old hoots."

Jack laughed. "They're young at heart, Annie. I hope we're like that someday."

"Like crazy old hoots?" Annie said, staring into his eyes.

"Just think, we'll have Ashton to chase us all over town." He started up the engine, looked over his shoulder, and slowly pulled away from the curb.

"We need more than Ashton. Boys can be so cold. We need a daughter. She'll be warm and kind and loving toward us old hoots."

Jack glanced over toward Annie and then turned his attention back to the road. "Little boys aren't cold. They're just not all that sensitive. They like to get dirty and talk loud."

"Well, our little Ashton is going to develop his sensitive side," Annie stated.

"I'm ready to expand our family anytime you are," Jack said.

Annie reached over and took his free hand into hers, gently squeezing it and causing him to look over at her. "Hey, keep all eyes on the road. Baby on board," she said teasingly.

CHAPTER SIX

Annie stood outside on the porch and drew in the smell of the warm wind coming off the intercoastal waterway. She watched as it reached the trees, whipping the branches around. She pulled her sweater in and clutched it closed with her hands. She reared her head back to keep the windblown stray hairs from falling into her eyes. She peered over her shoulder when she heard the screen door open.

Jack wrapped his arms around her waist. Pulling her close, Jack rested his chin on Annie's shoulder as they both looked out toward the dark sky.

"It's getting pretty bad out there," she said, leaning into him.

"The weatherman is saying that the brunt of the storm shouldn't come near us. We'll just have wind and heavy rain. I'm glad your grandmother and auntie are on their way. The Battery and all of downtown will flood after this one blows through."

"I know enough about these storms that they are not predictable. I hope all we get is some rain and wind," Annie said, turning toward Jack and giving him a quick kiss. "I'm going to go check the pantry."

She went into the kitchen to do a quick inventory. They'd been prepared for these types of storms before, but fortunately in all their years living in the area, only once did they suffer extreme hardship from a hurricane.

Jack peered into the playpen where Ashton slept. "He can sleep through anything, huh?" He winked at Annie.

"Men and boys," she said, raising an eyebrow.

"Wait, what does that mean?" he said, crossing to the kitchen with a cunning gaze on his face.

Annie crossed her arms and slanted her head slightly. "Let's see, you've slept through thunder and lightning and the time I was sicker than a dog and barfing my brains out in the bathroom. You sleep through Ashton's crying ..."

"Okay, I get it, but when I'm tired, I'm tired."

Annie furrowed her brows. "And women aren't?"

"You win, let's not argue about who is more attentive," Jack said, pulling her in close and sneaking a kiss.

"I was just looking and I think we have enough food and water to carry us for a few days," she said, trying to ignore his kisses.

"I have the generator all ready to go, if we need it." He gave her a quick kiss before he moved away.

"I hope we don't. I'm worried about Grandmother and Auntie. Don't you think they should have been here by now?"

Jack glanced at his watch. "Well, Charles said they were about to walk out the door, so yes, I do think they should be here. I'll call him on his cell."

Annie watched as she bit her bottom lip. Something didn't seem right about this, but she hoped, for once, her intuition would be wrong.

"Voice mail," Jack said, staring blankly at Annie.

"Probably because he's driving. I'll try Betsy," Annie said, reaching for her cell phone. She tapped her foot and then moved around the room with the phone glued to her ear. "Betsy, this is Annie. Just checking in on you, since we were expecting you a while ago. Call me."

"Voice mail?" Jack said.

Annie nodded.

"Okay, let's not get worried. They are with Charles and Betsy, who we feel are very responsible, or we wouldn't leave Lilly and Patty in their charge. Let's give them another half hour. The traffic is probably a nightmare coming out of the city. In the meantime, I'm going down to the dock to make sure *Lady Powell* is securely tied and do a quick assessment of our property."

Just then, Ashton screamed at the top of his lungs, and had them both rushing into the living room. There, he stood hanging onto the sides, jumping up and down, and laughing.

Annie shot Jack a terrified look and then reached down into the playpen and pulled Ashton into her arms. "Your first hurricane," she said, leaning in and kissing him on his chubby little cheeks. Ashton let out a belly laugh and then playfully rubbed off her wet kiss on his cheeks.

"And probably not your last, if you live here," Jack said. He lowered his mouth to Ashton's neck and blew a raspberry, making him giggle more.

Annie sunk into the cushiony sofa and bounced Ashton on her leg. She sang a little song she'd heard somewhere about the horsey went this way, and the horsey went that way, and then proceeded to pump her legs up and down as if he were riding a horse. His laughter was contagious, and soon Annie and Jack were laughing, too.

Jack picked up the remote and turned the volume up on the television. They both stared at the screen as they listened to the reports that this could be the largest storm to hit this part of the United States in twenty-five years. Annie breathed in and held her breath slightly. Her heart quickened as she listened.

"I'm going to gather all the candles and lighters and have them in one central place," she said, jumping up from the sofa and handing Ashton off to Jack.

"After you're done, I'm going to walk around the property and check on things one last time," Jack said.

As Annie raided the cupboards for the candles, flashlights, and a battery operated lantern, both Buffy and Isla followed her. "It's okay, guys. We'll be safe," she said, patting them each on the head. Isla wagged her tail at a slow speed, and Buffy looked on with her saucer-sized brown eyes. "I know, how about a treat?" She walked over to the pantry and retrieved the bag of chicken bites. She leaned over and gave each dog a bite. Now, their tails were wagging at lightning speed.

After she gathered all the lighting devices, she put them all in a pile on the dining table and headed back into the living room. She held out her hands to Ashton who held onto the coffee table. He let go one hand and then the other and took the two steps into his mother's arms.

"He'll be walking soon, then look out," Jack said as he rose from the couch and crossed into the kitchen. He removed his windbreaker from the back of the chair and put it on. He raised the hood over his head and tightly secured it.

"Be careful out there, Jack. I can hear the wind from inside here."

He leaned in and kissed her mouth. "I'm always careful."

Annie and Ashton played patty-cake and rode the pretend horsey again, but then she realized he hadn't eaten yet. "Let's have lunch," she said, picking him up and walking to the kitchen. She pulled out his high chair and placed him in it. She then began preparing his lunch and theirs.

He'd made quite the mess on his tray, and standing back with her hands on her hips, Annie wondered how much of it the dogs had consumed. Isla and Buffy both were mere inches from the high chair and wagging their tails. On the floor were pieces of food and on the tray were remnants of something smeared everywhere. She wet a paper towel and began to clean him and the surrounding area up, when she realized that Jack still hadn't returned from outside.

She pulled off the tray and picked up Ashton, heading to the back screened porch to see if she could find Jack. There was no sign of him. She opened the screen door to the outside, and leaned forward, straining her neck as far as she could, to see if there were any lights on in the garage, but it appeared dark.

"We better go find Daddy." She moved to the front of the house and opened the door that led to the wraparound porch. She shielded Ashton from the wind as she stepped out onto the porch. She called out Jack's name, but there was no answer. She walked to the end of the porch one way and looked around toward the back side of the house. She called his name once more —nothing. She hurriedly walked to the opposite end of the porch, where the huge magnolia tree stood, and peered as far as her eyes would take her—nothing again. She called his name, and again no response. Now her heart began to pound and a sick feeling hit her squarely in the stomach. She clutched Ashton to her bosom. "Where's daddy?" she whispered in his ear.

Trying to think fast and feeling a bit cumbersome with Ashton, she knew she only had one real choice. The two of them would have to brave the storm winds and look for Jack. She rushed back into the house and pulled Jack's little jacket from the closet and put it on him, covering his head with the hood. She tossed on her rain slicker and then the two stepped quickly back outside.

She immediately went down to the dock first. Something told her to look there first. She'd just cleared the first little hump that then took them down to the water, when she saw his body lying still on the dock.

"Jack," she screamed as she ran to his side, slipping and sliding while holding Ashton tightly in her arms. She leaned over and touched him, and then she shoved him. "Jack! Jack, wake up," she screamed.

Ashton began to cry as he tried to wiggle out of her grasp. Annie tried to protect him from the rain pelleting him in the face, but all eyes were on Jack.

"Jack, can you hear me?" Annie looked him over to see if she could see any wounds. She saw the gash on his head and the blood gushing from it. Jack moaned. "I'm going to run and get help, baby. Just hold on." Annie got up from her knees and looked back up the hill toward their home. "Vicky!" Annie called out in a high, petrified scream.

A dull rumbling in the hollow of her gut told her to run as fast as she could. Holding Ashton, she ran. The rain came down really hard now, and the wind about blew them both over. She kept running, though. She couldn't let anything happen to Jack. She ran over the little footbridge that crossed over the marsh area and headed straight over to Vicky and Scott's house. She pounded on their door until they opened it.

"Annie," Vicky shouted. "Come inside," she said, pulling them both in.

"Jack's been hurt. He's down at the bottom of the dock."

Scott came from the back room, and as he listened, he grabbed his raincoat off the coat tree. "I'll go. You guys stay here. Call 9-1-1 and tell them we have an emergency. Tell them to meet us at your house."

Annie and Vicky watched as Scott rushed out the front door. Vicky put her arm around Annie and pulled her close. "Don't worry, he has military training, and he'll get Jack to safety."

Vicky fixed them each a cup of hot tea, and while Ashton played on the floor with some coasters and wooden spoons, the girls sipped the warm spiced tea.

"I'm worried about Lilly and Patty, too. They were supposed to arrive well over an hour ago. We've called both Charles's and Betsy's cell phones, but they go straight into voice mail." Annie lowered her head and stared into her cup.

"Okay, I think we should call the highway patrol," Vicky said, getting her phone. "What kind of car are they driving?"

Annie listened on as Vicky gave the dispatcher all the information. No sooner had she hung up the phone than they heard the sounds of sirens.

"Ambulance," Annie said, pulling herself up from the sofa.

"Wait, let me call Scott."

Annie paced the room as she waited.

"Okay, he said the ambulance just pulled up. He's flagging them now."

Annie's eyes widened. She pictured Scott on the little hill waving like a madman, directing the ambulance crew to the dock.

"He'll call us after they get Jack into the ambulance. Just a few more minutes." Vicky rushed to Annie and pulled her in for a hug. "It's going to be all right. Just a few more minutes and we'll have a better update."

"I hate that I can't be there for Jack," Annie cried into Vicky's shoulder.

"I know, dear, but you'll be with him soon. The weather is just too awful for you to be out there. We don't need two injuries."

Annie nodded. Just then, Vicky's cell rang.

"Okay, he's stable, and they'll be approaching our house in a few minutes. You can ride with Jack in the back."

Annie's eyes settled on Ashton and then back to Vicky.

"Don't worry about him. We'll take great care of him."

Annie rushed over to Vicky and planted a kiss on her cheek and then did the same to Ashton. "Mommy will be back soon." She quickly stepped toward the front door, and looking back one last time at Ashton, she headed out the door. She'd been outside for less than thirty seconds when the ambulance pulled up. Scott bounded out from the back and waved his hands wildly at Annie to hurry up.

Annie pulled herself up into the back of the ambulance where Jack and two paramedics sat, one on each side of him. "Jack, Jack, it's Annie. I'm right here, darling," she said, taking his hand in hers and squeezing lightly. Jack's eyes fluttered, but he didn't make a single sound.

CHAPTER SEVEN

"Annie." He opened his arms wide and let her fall into his embrace.

"Please, tell me he's going to be okay," she said, choking back tears.

"He has a slight concussion, a fat lip, and a sprained wrist, but he's alive, and is going to be just fine," Dr. Carlisle said.

"I'm so happy you're the doctor on call today, Michael. How fortunate for him ... for us," Annie said with pleading eyes.

"Not the best timing, with the storm and all. How did Jack get hurt?"

"I'm not sure. He'll have to tell us, once he's awake. All I know is that he said he was going to check on the property and *Lady Powell*. When he didn't return, we went looking for him. I found him on the dock with blood coming from his head."

Michael patted her on the shoulder. "You can go in and see him. He was coming around when I was in there, so I expect him to be awake soon. Then you can drill him on what he was doing out in this awful weather."

Annie nodded. She sank her eyes to the floor and slowly made her way down the hall to his room. When she stepped inside, the stillness of the room made her shudder. Seeing poor Jack lying in his hospital bed made her sad, and she quickly wiped away the trailing tears. She picked up her pace and rushed to his bedside. She pulled up a chair and sat holding his hand, waiting for him to wake up.

After a few minutes of rubbing his thumb against hers, she rose and leaned over, kissing him on his mouth. His eyes fluttered a bit. "Jack, it's Annie," she whispered.

She traced his chest with her fingers and then sighing, she sat back down. She rested her cheek on his leg, muffling her cries into the sheet.

She reared her head up when she felt his fingers tangle up in her hair. "Jack," she said in a guarded tone, a partial smile crossing her mouth.

"Hey, baby," he said, barely audible.

Annie's half smile soon turned to a broad one. "I love you, Jack!"

A low chuckle made its way out of his mouth, bringing with it a quaint smile.

Annie leaned over and kissed him on the mouth. "Michael said you're going to be okay. You just have a little bump on the head and a sprained wrist."

Jack groaned as he tried to lift his head.

"Let me help," Annie said, grabbing the bed remote and lifting the head for him. She fluffed his pillow, straightened his bedding, and poured him some fresh water.

He planted his hands on each side and moved his body up a bit, peering at her through half-closed eyes. "How long was I knocked out?"

"I'm not sure. When Ashton and I found you, you weren't out, but just dazed."

"I don't remember much."

"That's okay, you rest. Maybe it will come to you later."

Jack's eyes flew open. "The hurricane! Ashton, your grandmother, and Patty."

"Everyone is okay. Ashton is with Scott and Vicky. Grandmother and Patty, along with Charles and Betsy, are all at your parents' house."

Jack shook his head a few times. "Huh? Scott and Vicky, my parents ..." he said, drifting off.

"Don't worry about anything. I'll explain later. Right now, you rest and get better. We need you home." She patted him on the arm.

Just then the hospital door flew open and in walked a nurse, pushing a cart along. "Time to take his vitals," she sang.

Annie backed away, while the nurse did her job. "I'll be right back. Just going to make a call," she said, showing her cell phone and waving it around to the nurse.

"How's my little buddy doing?" Annie asked her friend, once she answered.

"He's fine," Vicky reassured her. "He's playing with Scott's keys, and whatever else we can find to entertain him. Scott did run back over to your house and grabbed the dogs ... and some diapers."

"Oh, Vicky, that's so nice of you all. I wanted to update you on Grandmother and Auntie. They made it over to Milly and Robert's, and I guess they're having a big old hurricane party!"

Vicky laughed into the phone. "Man, see what we are missing because Jack fell on his head?"

"I know, right? I guess Grandmother and Auntie are

in sheer delight being over there. Jack's grandparents are there, too."

"I can only imagine what poor Milly is going through. She's probably pulling her hair out."

"I talked to Mary. She and Danny are over there, too. I guess they're making margaritas and all this food before the power goes out."

"If the power goes out," Vicky corrected.

"How are the winds?"

"They've actually died down some, but you know what they say ..."

"The calm before the storm?" Annie pulled her bottom lip in.

"Let's think positive. So what's your plan?"

"Jack's going to insist I leave to be with Ashton. I don't know how dangerous that will be. I'm going to check with the guards here, and see if I can get any more updates about the news before I make my decision. Jack is out of the woods and just requires rest. He's safe here."

"Okay, well whatever you do, let us know before you do it."

Annie agreed to Vicky's terms and then bid her good-bye. She walked down the hallway that led to the reception desk, and spoke with the volunteers who were manning it. They gave her all the details they had on the storm and then directed her to watch the news. She moseyed over to the seating area, where she sat, taking in the weather reports. She spotted a Keurig machine in the corner and popped back up, making her way over to fix herself a cup of coffee. She kept her eyes and ears on the television as the coffee dripped into her cup. Taking her cup, she drew in the smell of the fresh coffee, while she listened to the latest. Apparently, the worst of the storm had blown over. Just like a lot of these storms, it had fizzled out before it came ashore, but not before it brought minimal flooding to the downtown area and a few isolated power outages. This storm would go down in history as being minor. Letting out a sigh of relief, Annie took herself and her cup of coffee back to Jack's room to tell him the good news.

With Jack sleeping soundly, Annie didn't want to wake him, and instead leaned over and kissed him good-bye. "I'll be back. I'm going to go be with our little boy," she whispered, kissing him once again. She pulled up and began to move when he caught her hand with his. "Oh, you're awake."

"I'm drifting in and out. Michael said I'd be doing that for a while."

Annie raised her brow. "He came in, then? Michael saw you?"

Jack nodded. "Said that next time I want attention, I

should try asking for it, instead of falling in a storm and hitting my head, knocking myself unconscious."

Annie laughed. "He did, huh? Well, for the record, it was a little dramatic, I must say." She squeezed his hand.

"Ho ho ho," he mocked.

"Listen, good news, the storm is passing, and I can be with Ashton. Michael said he's keeping you overnight, so I'll be back tomorrow to get you, okay?"

"Sounds good. Give my boy a big hug from his accident-prone daddy."

"Jack?" Annie said, tilting her head to the right.

Jack blinked and then nodded.

"How did the accident happen? Do you have any recollection now?"

Jack brushed his hand through his hair. "Yeah, I went to bend over to tug on the rope for the boat, and I guess a gust of wind came up and slammed me down on the deck, head first. I managed to roll over onto my back, but then realized my wrist was hurting badly. I then blanked out. Really, when you think about it, it shouldn't have knocked me out, but I guess I'm a lightweight."

"No, you're not a lightweight. The wind was forceful. It was like dropping a couple of hundred pounds on a wooden surface. You might have hit your head on something before falling, and just don't realize it."

Jack drew in a long breath and let it out loudly. "Well, whatever the case may be, I'm going to be okay, and except for a sprained wrist and bruised pride, I'll be home tomorrow." He winked at her, causing her to smile.

"I'm going to call a cab. Know any good drivers who are willing to brave some rain?" she coyly asked.

"Call Richard."

"Yeah, I can't do that."

"Why not?"

"Because, while you were lying on a dock bleeding, and then rushed to the hospital, those guys were having a hurricane party."

Jack's eyes widened.

"Fortunately, Grandmother and Auntie made it there, too." Annie shook her head side to side.

"Oh, your family fits in so well with mine," he said, chuckling.

Annie leaned over and placed her mouth on his. His lips felt dry, probably from being out in the elements for so long. She breathed in his scent, but instead of the earthy sensual aroma she'd normally get from a combination of his shower gel, deodorant, and their laundry detergent, Annie took in the smell of bleached linen, dried blood, and rubbing alcohol. She wrinkled her nose.

"I'll check with Michael on the way out, to find out

what time to pick you up tomorrow. Get some rest. I have a feeling we'll have some cleanup to do out at Sweet Magnolia."

"What about the bakery?" Jack asked.

Annie began to wobble, her eyes growing to the size of saucers. She'd forgotten all about her beloved little cupcakery. She pulled in her bottom lip to try and stop it from quivering.

"Now, Annie, don't get worked up about the bakery. It's probably just fine," Jack said, trying to calm the second storm brewing.

Annie pulled out her phone and dialed a number. "I need to find a way back to Vicky and Scott's. Who over there hasn't been drinking and can come get me?"

"Robert. We'll send him," Mary said.

Annie could hear all the chatter coming from the Powell household. She swore she could hear Grandmother's cackle from a distance. She pursed her lips. "Okay, please tell him to hurry."

Annie sat back down near Jack's bed. "Your dad is coming to get me." She bent over, retrieving her purse, and slipped her phone inside. "I guess he's the only one who hasn't tasted the juice, yet." She smiled broadly and then reached out and slid her hand up and down his arm.

"I can't wait to get out of this hospital bed and go home." He dropped his head back onto the pillow.

"Soon, babe, soon."

Annie looked up when Robert entered the hospital room. He rushed over to Jack and patted his leg. "Son, are you ok?"

"Just a little sore. I'll be all right," Jack answered.

"How did this happen?" Robert pulled up a chair beside the bed and sat.

"I went down to the dock to check on *Lady Powell*. A gust of wind knocked me right on my butt."

"He hit his head on something and was knocked out," Annie said, cutting in.

Robert nodded. "Well, do what the doctors tell you to do." He stood.

Annie stood as well and leaned over the bed, kissing Jack on the forehead. "I'll be back tomorrow to get you." She stepped back and a slow smile quirked her face.

"Bye, babe." His forlorn look and disappointing tone told her he wasn't looking forward to sleeping at the hospital.

"Get some rest." She blew him a kiss as she exited his room.

CHAPTER EIGHT

"Thanks so much for picking me up, Robert." Annie buckled her seat belt.

"No worries, glad to be of help. You sure you don't want to come back to the house?"

Annie shook her head. "I want to go get Ashton. He's probably confused and wondering what happened to Jack."

Robert nodded, keeping eyes on the road. Now, the rain was coming down even heavier.

"So much for the storm passing us," she said, peering out the window.

"Said by eight o'clock tonight, it would be moving up the coast and eventually going out to sea."

"Those clouds look so ominous, though," she said,

stretching her neck to see them, a tone of worry in her voice.

"We aren't out of the woods yet for tornados. That's a real probability. Why don't you pick up Ashton and the dogs and come back to the house?"

Annie turned her head and stared at her father-in-law. He was one of the sweetest men she'd ever met—except Jack, of course. "Okay, that sounds good," she said, almost whispering.

Traffic came to a standstill on more than one occasion, but Robert had the patience of Job. Annie muttered a few unladylike words under her breath, but not Robert, who remained calm. He weaved in and out of cars with such ease, and never once did she hear any four-letter words from him. After a grueling ninety minutes, they pulled up to Vicky and Scott's.

She unbuckled her seat belt. "I'll just be a minute." She bounded out of the car and headed to their front door.

Annie rushed to Ashton and picked him up, pecking kisses all over his face and head. "Mommy is here. I told you I'd be back."

"How's Jack?" Vicky asked.

"He's doing well. Michael was the doctor on duty. Can you believe it? He said he should be good as new and discharged tomorrow. Robert, Jack's dad, is waiting for me out in the car. We're going to go over to their house for dinner."

"He was a little doll. He's so precious. I know he missed you, but he was so good," Vicky said, stroking his little head.

"Thank you," Annie mouthed before she leaned in and kissed her friend on the cheek.

"Yep, makes us want to have kids of our own," Scott yelled from across the room, sitting on the overstuffed armchair with Buffy on his lap and Isla down at his feet.

Annie shook her head when she saw her lazy pooches. "I see they got comfortable pretty quickly," she said, motioning to the dogs.

Scott chuckled. "They're good dogs. You have a great kid and good dogs. Now, that husband of yours ..." He chuckled some more.

Annie smiled. "I think you'd make great parents. And I think you should get a dog. Every child needs a pet ..." she said trailing off, realizing she may have hit a delicate spot with them. Annie hoped and prayed they would succeed in adopting. Scott and Vicky could give a child everything they'd ever dreamed about, and more. "Okay, guys, thanks again. Love you both," she said, waving to them as she made her way to the front door.

"Be careful out there. The rain is coming down in

buckets," Scott said as he approached the entryway, with Isla and Buffy following him.

"Robert is the safest driver I know, besides Jack." She winked. Annie hightailed it out the front door, shielding little Ashton as best as she could. She opened the back seat, and the two dogs jumped in. Holding Ashton on her lap, she said, "We need to go to our house. I need to get some dry clothes, diapers, and his car seat."

Robert pulled the car up front so Annie could stay as dry as possible.

"I'll be as quick as I can."

Annie grabbed the diaper bag and stuffed it with diapers, wipes, some finger foods, his sippy cup, and a bottle–just in case. She opened the drawers to his dresser and tossed a footed sleeper and another change of clothes into the bag. She sighed. "I must be forgetting something, but what?" Then it dawned on her—a phone charger. Her battery showed it was at less than twenty-five percent.

She ran out of the house and heaved herself into the front seat, breathing heavily. Grandpa held Ashton while he messed around with the steering wheel. She brushed her wet hair back with her hands. "I need to get the car seat out of my car. Can you drive around back?"

After a few minutes of struggling with the car seat, Annie finally got it out of her car and into Robert's.

Little Ashton rode in the middle with Isla and Buffy on each side. He occasionally let out a giggle, causing Annie to look back. She laughed out loud. Isla and Buffy were licking the drops of water off of him.

"Smells like wet dog in here," Robert said, wrinkling his nose.

ROBERT HELPED BY GATHERING THE DOGS AND GRABBING the diaper bag. Annie had Ashton. They headed inside the house. Immediately, Annie could hear music and a sudden bellow of laughter, along with chattering going on.

"This must be the place where the party is," she said.

Robert nodded. "It's never a dull moment around here. Throw in a hurricane, and you have to celebrate." He held out his hand to take Annie's jacket. She wiggled out of one arm, while she transferred Ashton to her hip, then she positioned him to the other side so she could get the other arm out.

"Annie," Mary sang as she wrapped her arms around her and kissed Ashton.

"Mary," Annie said with a little wariness in her voice.

"Come join the party. We have food, drink—"

"I hear. It sounds like it's a great one. Too bad Jack isn't here," she said, cutting her off in a lofty tone.

Mary stepped back and eyed her sister. "We're all sorry that Jack got hurt. This party is not about celebrating him not being here. Take a chill pill, Sis."

Annie softened her features. A tear welled up. "I know, I'm sorry. I shouldn't have bitten off your face like that. It's been a trying few hours." She pulled Mary back into her embrace. "I think I could use a stiff drink to mellow out."

"Grandmother and Auntie are having a great time. They love Jack's grandparents."

Annie nodded. "Have you heard any news about the downtown area? I was wondering about the bakery."

"Annie," Milly shouted, rushing to her side and taking Ashton out of her arms, interrupting the sisters' conversation. "My little Ashton," she said, nuzzling his neck and blowing raspberries.

Mary stepped around Milly and placed her arm on Annie's shoulder. "Just some flooding, but I think it's minimal. We should be able to go check things out tomorrow. Milly is setting us all up here for the night. You're staying the night, too, right?"

Annie nodded. "Yes, I guess so. I promised to pick up Jack tomorrow. I guess I'll figure out all the logistics tomorrow. But right now, someone fix me a margarita. And make it a large one!"

ANNIE GREW TIRED OF REPEATING THE STORY ABOUT HOW she found Jack at the bottom of the hill, lifeless and bleeding. She'd just as soon forget about it. Ashton began to act fussy, so after feeding him and giving him a warm bath, Annie set him up in the portable crib that had belonged to Jack and his sister way back when, in Jack's old bedroom, which was now turned into a guest room. She bid the group good night, and then taking a nice long shower, she slipped into one of Jack's tee shirts she found in his old dresser and climbed into bed. The two large margaritas rimmed with salt relaxed her, and soon her eyes grew heavy with sleep, sweeping her away into dreamland.

SHE WOKE TO A LITTLE SOMEONE SCREECHING AT THE TOP of his lungs. She rubbed the sleep out of her eyes and focused on Ashton, who held on to the side of the crib, bouncing up and down, drooling all over the side, and laughing.

"Okay, little guy, give me a moment to clear my head." Annie stretched and yawned and then rolled her head to the side to see the time on the clock radio that was on the side table. She pushed off the covers, and placing one foot on the floor and then the other, she made her way over to Ashton. She reached in and pulled him into her arms. She kissed his forehead. "Ready to eat breakfast?" He cooed in her arms in response.

Annie searched the closet for something to put on over her skimpy tee shirt. She found an oversize sweatshirt from Jack's football days and a pair of even baggier sweatpants. A quick look in the mirror attached to the door caused her to scowl. "Yikes, I'm a sight for sore eyes." She brushed her ratty hair down, and the two exited the bedroom, making their way to the kitchen.

As she approached the alcove into the kitchen area, she could hear Grandmother, Auntie, and Milly talking.

"Good morning, everyone," she said cheerfully, making eye contact with each of them.

"Good morning, dear," Patty said.

"How'd you sleep?" Milly asked.

Annie pulled a coffee cup off of the cup tree and poured herself a cup of coffee. With Ashton on her hip, she pulled the refrigerator door open and searched for cream and something to give him for breakfast.

"I slept well. Ashton is hungry," she peered over the top of the refrigerator door and made eye contact with Milly.

"How about some scrambled eggs?" Milly rose from her chair and crossed over to where Annie stood.

"I can make them. That sounds good." Annie dropped her head back inside and grabbed the carton of eggs.

"Here, let me hold him, then," Milly said, opening her arms to accept Ashton.

Annie passed him over to his grandma and proceeded to make bacon, eggs, and cheese grits. The smell of the sizzling bacon soon had everyone up.

The lively conversation around the table brought a small secret smile to Annie's face. Being part of this large family brought such joy, to not only her, but to Grandmother and Auntie.

Annie pulled the cup close to her lips, about to draw a sip of coffee, when the house phone rang. Robert answered it with a deep, "Hello." Annie watched as Robert carried on a conversation with the party on the line. He then motioned for her to get the phone. "It's Jack. He's chomping at the bit to come home," he said, laughing in exhilaration as he handed her the phone.

"Jack! Are you ready to come home, dear?"

"Yes, I've been calling your cell."

"I'm sorry. We're just finishing up breakfast here. Has Michael made it in to see you already?"

"Yes, and I'm cleared to resume my duties as your loving husband."

Annie sniggered. "Okay, then let me get dressed, and we'll come get you."

"We'll?"

"I had your dad bring us over, so I don't have the car. I'll get your dad to bring me to the hospital."

"Okay, see you in a bit."

Annie hung up the phone and then turned around. All eyes and ears were on her. She smiled and then brushed her hair back onto her shoulders. "That was Jack. He's ready to come home ..." she sputtered, feeling a bit embarrassed with all the attention on her right then.

Robert stood. "Okay, let's go get him."

"I need to get dressed first. If you all could finish feeding Ashton, I'll run up to the room to change and get our things." She bolted out of the room and took two stairs at a time. She pushed open the bedroom door and quickly changed.

~

"Now, take it easy, Jack," Robert said, helping him into the car.

"I'm good, Dad, really," Jack said.

Robert shook his head. "Boy, you're so hardheaded. You must have gotten that from your mother's side."

Jack shot his dad a puzzled look and then broke out into a sudden and happy laugh.

Robert helped them inside, and after he left, they put Ashton in his playpen to play.

"It's so good to be home," Jack said, pulling Annie in for a kiss. His lips brushed against hers lightly, sending chills up her spine and the hairs on her arms to stand. He'd only been away from her for a day, but it felt like more. She kissed him back, barely gazing at his lips. After a few moments, she applied feather light pressure to let him know she enjoyed it, and didn't want him to stop. He pulled her into his embrace tighter now, brushing his hands through her hair and rubbing her arms in an up and down motion. He held her back for a moment, gazing hard into her eyes. He dropped his voice to a whisper. "I love you, Annie."

"I love you, too." She moved closer, their lips once

more touching. The mere presence of him caused her stomach to clench tight.

"I'll always love you, no matter what. I hope you know that." He dropped a kiss on her forehead.

"In sickness and health, that's what our vows said. I will honor them until the day I die." She gazed lovingly into his eyes.

He brushed back the strand of hair that fell across her eye and then cupped her head with his hands. He leaned in and then hesitated briefly. She inched closer toward him, taking in his sweetness. They moved in at the same time, their lips touching. She let out a soft moan when he pressed her mouth open. She accepted his hunger as she weaved her hands through his hair, holding on to him like the anchor he was to her.

CHAPTER NINE

T he hurricane spared Charleston, and except for several inches of rain, which caused some minor flooding, the city bounced back fairly quickly. The bakery, as well as several businesses along the downtown area, had lost power, which resulted in the necessity to toss out a few perishable items, but overall, Sweet Indulgence came out of the storm unscathed.

Sweet Magnolia, the Powell residence, not so much. The cleanup took several days and consisted of many downed tree limbs and some debris which had blown in from outer areas. Jack even found a fender to some car, from who knows where, stuck up high in a tree branch. Both Annie and Jack were surprised, but very happy that the magnolia where they had taken their vows still stood stately and strong. Not one single limb had come down during that storm. Unfortunately, *Lady Powell* suffered quite a bit of damage.

"Oh, Jack, I'm so sorry," Annie said, nodding toward *Lady Powell,* whose bottom half had sunk due to a hole the size of a watermelon found on her stern.

Jack brushed his hand through his hair. "This is going to cost big bucks to fix."

"Is it fixable?"

"I think so, but who knows? The boat shop will be able to tell us."

"Don't worry, Jack. If she can't be repaired and made seaworthy, we'll buy a new boat. Our insurance should cover that."

"Oh, yeah, it will. It's just that this boat has so many memories ..."

Annie wrapped her arms around his waist. "I know." She nuzzled his neck, recalling their steamy kisses and much more on that boat.

"I've taken this boat clear down the intercoastal waterway to Myrtle Beach and beyond."

Annie nodded. "And we've had some great times in this boat," she said, urging him to remember along with her.

"And fishing trips—Richard and my dad ... well, we've been fishing from one end of this bay to the other."

"I know, *Lady Powell* means the world to you. Remember when we took Grandmother and Auntie on their first trip?"

"And during some of my deepest sorrows, this boat has brought me many hours of joy and happiness."

"Okay, I get it, *Lady Powell* has been there for you when no one else has, but she's pretty special to me, too," Annie said, clearly irritated with Jack.

Jack raised a brow and stared hard at Annie. "If I didn't know better, I'd say someone was jealous of my relationship with her," he said, nodding toward the boat.

Annie sputtered a word or two before she got going. "No ... not ... at ... all. It's just that for a second, I felt like I was attending some wake or funeral. She is a boat."

Jack overexaggerated a gasp and his hand flew to his mouth. "Just a boat?" He let out a loud roar of laughter and then pulled her in close for a hug.

"Jack Powell, you're messing with me."

"You're darn right I am. And if you're going to make it so easy to fall into my trap, I'll do it every time." He kissed her forehead, then held her back and stared into her eyes. "You know I love you and Ashton more than *Lady Powell*, don't you?"

Annie let her gaze fall. "Yes," she whispered.

"Okay, then, let's go back to the house. I have a few calls to make so we can decide the fate of the old girl.

Maybe it's time to get a new boat and make all new memories," he said, leading the way back toward the house on the hill, Sweet Magnolia.

THE HUGE TOWBOAT CAME AND FETCHED *LADY POWELL* out of the water. Annie stayed on the porch with Ashton and the dogs. Jack slowly made his way to the house, his head hanging low. Annie gulped the lump down in her throat, her pulse rising a bit in anticipation of what she'd say to him.

"She's gone," he said, making his way up the steps. He held out his arms and took Ashton.

"I'm sorry, babe. Maybe they can repair her. We'll wait for final word."

TO KEEP BUSY, JACK WENT BACK TO WORK AT THE woodshop, and Annie to the bakery. Milly picked up right where she'd left off in terms of watching Ashton for them. Annie found herself becoming less involved with the day-to-day operation of Sweet Indulgence. She'd hired wonderful staff and they were performing great. She'd pop in a couple of days a week, but truth be told, they'd just as soon wish she weren't there. "Sometimes, the boss can hinder job performance," she overheard one of them saying. And with Betsy cutting her hours back to almost nothing to care for Grandmother and Auntie, Annie almost felt like a stranger in her own bakery.

"Greetings, everyone," she said, waving to Peter in the kitchen.

"Hey, Ms. Annie," Toby said.

"Hello, Toby. Just you today? Where's Keith at?" She didn't even know who was on the schedule these days.

"Peter has him scheduled to come in later today."

Annie nodded as she made her way around the counter. "Has it been slow today?"

"A little. It will pick up later when the college kids come in. They sleep later." A wide-toothed grin spread across his face.

Annie stepped into the kitchen. She took in the wonderful smell of flour, sugar, and baked goodies. "I love the smell of cupcakes," she said, peering into the ovens.

"Chocolate chip, banana crème, and my new favorite, heath." Peter continued to mix ingredients, not looking up at Annie.

"Heath?"

"It's a vanilla based batter with little bits of toffee

and chocolate. The icing is a butterscotch crème. It's really popular."

"Did you come up with this new flavor all by yourself?"

Peter stopped cleaning off the beaters and slowly rose. Squaring his shoulders, he smiled. "Yep."

"Brilliant," Annie said.

"I wanted to ask you about hiring some more workers," he said.

"Oh?"

"Keith can't work as many hours anymore. He's on the schedule for ten this week, and six next. Toby and I have been covering counter duty."

"That's not good. Okay, let's run another ad. Do you want me to set up interviews?" She surprised herself by falling into the employee, and not the boss, frame of mind. "I mean, I probably should set up the interviews," she corrected.

"Whatever, no worries," Peter said, getting back to work.

Annie felt strange about how the conversation had gone and how she felt standing in her once favorite spot in the entire world. Marriage and motherhood had changed her. She slowly made her way out of the kitchen and glanced around the bakery. Just as Toby had predicted, customers were beginning to come in. She whispered goodbye and then retreated from the bakery. Breathing heavily, she stood with her back against the brick portion of the outside and clutched her chest. A tear rolled down her face, and she quickly brushed it away. Then, she briskly walked to her parked car and drove hurriedly to Milly's. For some unexplained reason, she had a strong yearning to see Ashton ... and Jack.

CHAPTER TEN

"Well, this is a pleasant surprise," Milly said, opening the door wide with Ashton on her hip.

Annie reached her arms out, and Ashton laughingly slid right into his mommy's arms. Annie nuzzled his neck, then kissed him on the cheek. "I missed my boy," she said, her eyes misting a little.

"Come in. Tell me how you're feeling today. I sense a bit of an emotional roller coaster going on," Milly said, leading the way to the kitchen.

Annie sighed loudly.

"Cinnamon and rose, or rose and lavender?"

"Either sounds delightful," Annie said, sliding out a chair at the kitchen table and sitting down.

While the two waited for the water to boil, Milly

rested her backside against the cabinetry. She tilted her head and furrowed her brows. "What's going on, honey?"

"I don't know. All of a sudden, I've lost interest in Sweet Indulgence, or maybe it's the workers have lost interest in me. I miss Ashton while I'm there, and have trouble concentrating. Maybe I'm not the modern woman of today, after all." Annie lowered her mouth to the top of Ashton's head and kissed him lightly.

"These are normal feelings you're having. Ask any new mother, and they'll tell you." Milly went to work preparing the cups of tea.

"I know, but this feels different. It's as if my purpose in life has changed."

"Maybe it has, but don't do anything drastic."

"I won't," Annie said, feeling defeated.

"Listen," Milly brought the cups over and pulled out a chair. "Why don't you give it a few days? Think over about what it is you really want. Talk to Jack. He'll tell you exactly how he feels about it. Then make the decision together." Milly brought one of the cups to her mouth and blew. "I love the smell of this lavender rose one." She drew in a small taste.

Annie picked up her cup and copied Milly. "Cinnamon, yum."

"I think I would be just as happy being the owner

and just overseeing the cupcakery that way. I have my hands full with being a mom and wife. I don't need to be running a business right now." Ashton began to wiggle on his mom's lap and tried to get down. "He'll be walking soon. Then, you'll have your hands full, and I don't think that's fair to you. You've raised your family, and you've helped with watching Crystal for Richard and Diane."

Milly nodded her head. "True, and I have loved every minute of it." She drew in another taste of her tea.

"We want to have another child," Annie blurted out.

Milly put the cup down hard on the table. "Are you ...?"

"No, but we're trying." A wide smile spread across Annie's face.

"A little brother or sister for Ashton," Milly said, reaching over and playfully grabbing his leg.

Ashton let out a shrill scream that made both Annie and Milly laugh.

"Well, it sounds like you know what you have to do, my dear. You'll make the right decision."

While Ashton played with his Cheerios on his high

chair top, Annie prepared Jack's favorite dinner. She'd just peeked in the oven, when he entered the house.

"Something smells wonderful," he said, first kissing Ashton then hugging Annie.

"I made your favorite."

"What's the occasion?" He peered inside the oven and took in a deep whiff of the roast with carrots and potatoes.

Annie shrugged her shoulders. "No special occasion."

Jack started to head back to the bedroom but stopped quickly. He placed both hands on her arms and stared deeply into her eyes. "You're not ... we're not ..."

Annie laughed and shook her head vehemently. "No, not yet, but I do want to discuss something with you."

"Let me jump in the shower and wash off all the wood dust. Hold that thought." He leaned in and dropped a kiss on her mouth.

"Dinner will be ready in twenty," she yelled as he ran down the hallway.

Annie plated slices of tender roast, spoonfuls of cooked carrots and potatoes, and carried them to the table Jack made. She placed one of the plates in front of Jack. She cut up the carrots and mashed the cubes of potatoes and put them on a child's plate and placed it on Ashton's high chair tray.

Jack clasped his hands first, and then Annie followed. "Thank you, Father, for this food we're about to eat, and thank you for keeping my family safe from the hurricane. Amen."

"Amen," Annie repeated.

Their prayers were always simple but well intended.

Jack sampled a piece of the tender meat, while Annie coaxed Ashton into eating. She finally took a bite of the food. "The meat is so tender. I bet Ashton could eat some of this, too." She offered him a bite. He wiggled in his seat after he tasted it.

"I think he likes it," Jack said, shoveling the food in, one bite after another.

Annie smiled. "Are you starving?"

"I didn't get lunch today, so yes, I am." He took another bite of the food, then leaned back in his chair. "If you keep making dinners like this, I'm going to gain weight. It's a good thing you have a job that keeps you out of the kitchen, well, at least out of our kitchen," he joked.

Annie drew in her bottom lip and bit down. "Well, about that ..."

Jack leaned forward and put his fork down. "What happened? Did something happen to the bakery?" A worried look traversed his face as he waited for Annie to answer.

Annie swallowed down the lump that tried to take up residence in her throat, with a sip of her water. "I've been thinking about stepping back from the business."

Jack nodded as he tried to follow her train of thought. "Go on."

"They seem to be doing well without me. I'm going to hire a few more workers, though."

"Okay," Jack said, stretching out the word.

"I miss Ashton," Annie blurted.

"Now, we're getting somewhere," Jack said, smiling.

"And we are planning on having another baby. I don't think it's fair to your mother ... who's raised her children, to have to raise ours, too."

Jack cocked his head and pulled his brows in. "Did Mom say she didn't want to watch him?"

"No, no she'd never say that. I'm saying that. I just don't think it's fair to her."

"Annie, if you want to sell the business, you can. I'm for whatever you want. You know that, right?" Jack reached over and touched her hand with his.

Annie's eyes lowered to his hand. "I know," she whispered.

"What do you want to do?"

"I think I'll just be the owner. I'll drop in once a month or so. Just so that they don't forget about me. I'm going to make Peter supervisor, as well as a lead baker.

We'll get some more help for him so he can mainly concentrate on baking and scheduling employees. I can order the supplies for him, right here from our home computer."

"Sounds like you've got it all worked out." He laced his fingers with hers and gently squeezed her hand. "As I said, anything you want, I want it, too."

"The other bit of news I have is regarding Mary and Danny."

Jack withdrew his hand and began eating his dinner again.

"Aren't you interested in what I have to say about them?"

"I already know. They want to get married and live in the cottage."

Annie fell back against the chair and gasped. "Well ... what do you think about all of that?"

"Well, I told Danny that the cottage was intended for Lilly and Patty, but since they are too stubborn about moving out of their own home, and it sits empty, why not? I did tell him that I'd have to ask you, first." He winked at Annie as he forked another piece of the meat.

"You men, you already had it all decided. Here, Mary and I thought that we could be sneaky about something." Annie crossed her arms over her chest as she tightened her lips.

"What do you think? Can you have Mary living so close?

"Mary? How about Danny?" Annie uncrossed her arms and began to feed Ashton again.

Jack nodded. "True that." He lifted some carrots onto his fork and then ate them.

"We'd have to lay down some rules. Get it in writing," Annie continued.

Jack tipped his head toward her. "It hardly ever works out when you rent to family, though."

"Rent? I told Mary they could live there rent-free."

"What? I told Danny one thousand dollars a month, including utilities."

They both dropped their forks and stared at each other.

"Now what?" they both said at the same time.

CHAPTER ELEVEN

"Hey, Mary, what are you doing?" Annie asked in a chipper tone, while twirling her hair around her finger.

"Just finished going for a run with Danny. His therapist said exercise is one of the best things for his anxiety."

"That's great, Mary. Listen, I need to talk to you about something."

"Is it Grandma or Auntie Patty?"

"No," Annie said, trying to think fast on her feet.

"It's not Jack, or Ashton ... or you, is it? You're doing okay, right?"

"No, we're all fine," she said, delaying the real reason for her call. "I wanted to know if you wanted to have lunch with me." *Why was it so hard to just tell her the truth?* "I thought we could discuss your wedding plans."

Mary let out a long and overexaggerated gasp. "Thank goodness. Things have been going along so well, I couldn't take someone being ill. Unless it was from morning sickness," she said teasingly.

"No, no morning sickness ... yet."

"Yet!?"

"I'm just kidding. You'll be the third person to know, when it happens."

"Okay, lunch sounds good, but let's go for a drive first. I'll pick you up around eleven thirty. I want to show you something."

Annie raised her brow as she took in the mysterious tone in Mary's voice. She was up to something. "Okay, I'll be ready."

"Did you tell her?" Jack said, startling Annie.

Annie turned to face Jack and crossed her arms. "No, we're going to have lunch today. She wants to show me something first, though. I have no idea what is up her sleeve. You never know with Mary."

Jack stepped closer and wrapped his arms around her waist, causing her to drop her arms to her side. She looked at his scraggly two-day growth on his face. "When are you going to shave this off?" She ran her fingers across the scratchy patch.

Jack ran his hand along his jaw. "Don't you like it?"

Annie knitted her brows as she searched his face, studying it in more depth. "I'm not sure. It's kind of scratchy right now, maybe after it grows out."

Jack pulled her quickly against his chest and planted a kiss on her mouth. Annie's snicker soon turned into a soft groan as he smothered her with his juicy lips. She fell into his warm mouth and parted her lips for him. His kisses were simply the best.

With his hands on her arms now, Jack gently pushed away and stared into her eyes. "How's that for an I love you kiss?"

Annie beamed.

"Okay, so I have Ashton today, and you and Mary go out and have a great time."

Annie took a few steps toward Jack and reached for his hands. She playfully laced her fingers with his, while swinging their hands to and fro. "I love you, Jack. You're so good for me."

"We're good for each other." He dropped a kiss on the top of her head. "Now, go get ready for your lunch date with Mary."

Annie turned to head toward the hall, and Jack playfully swatted her bottom. She turned quickly and scowled. "Remember, I'll pay you back when you least expect it." She continued to the bedroom to get ready, chuckling all the way.

~

"WHERE ARE YOU TAKING ME?" ANNIE ASKED AS MARY traveled down a long gravel and dirt road, through a grove of huge oak trees draped in moss.

Mary shot her a grin. "It's a secret."

Annie tightened her lips as she stared out the windshield. Soon, a small white building came into view.

Mary pulled in and turned the motor off. "This is what I wanted to show you." She nodded toward the tiny structure.

"A worn down church? I mean, I think it's a church. It has a steeple on the top. What is this place, Mary?"

"This is on the historical register as being one of the oldest churches in this county."

"So?" Annie said, letting her know that her idea was not only preposterous, but downright idiotic.

"It started out as a one-room schoolhouse. Isn't that cool?" Mary opened her door. "Come on," she pleaded. She stood and stretched her arms as she waited for Annie to join her.

Annie reluctantly got out of the car and crossed over to where Mary stood. "You're serious? This is where you want to get married? Out in the middle of nowhere, in a one-room schoolhouse?"

"Don't be such a fuddy-duddy. This is really a cool place. They still use it for special occasions. What is more special than Danny and my wedding?" She grabbed Annie's hand and sprinted toward the door, dragging Annie behind.

They climbed the few steps leading to the porch. Mary dug into her pocket, and producing a key, she waved it in Annie's face. She unlocked the door and pushed it open. Annie followed Mary inside.

"Isn't this just great?" Mary skipped up the aisle to the front of the church. "We can have vases of flowers here on either side; we can have ribbons and bows on the pews. Grandmother and Auntie will be so happy that I get married in a church. They are still talking about your outdoor wedding."

Annie cut Mary a scowl. "What? They loved my wedding." Annie frowned, and then paused. "Didn't they?"

Mary ran back toward Annie and hugged her. "Yes, they loved your wedding. They just mentioned that they would have loved to see you get married in a church like Rebecca did."

Annie raised her shoulders up and down and sighed. "I can never please those women."

"Don't think about them. This makes up for Danny and me living in sin." Mary let out a loud laugh.

"Well, at least Jack and I didn't do that."

"Don't tell me you didn't try out the merchandise before you tied the knot, Ms. Annie." Mary shot her a wild grin.

Annie raised her chin and looked behind Mary, toward the front of the church. "I think your idea of flowers on either side would bring some color to this rather drab interior. It's so dark and gloomy."

"That's because the shutters are closed. We'll liven this place up. Plus, there's plenty of parking; it's a great location. Come on, Annie, tell me you like it," Mary said, begging for her approval.

Annie relaxed her shoulders, even though she still felt tense about Grandmother and Auntie not approving of her outdoor wedding. "I approve."

Mary wrapped her arms around Annie and picked her up and swung her around. Mary leaned back just a tad too far, and they both went crumbling down onto the wooden floor.

"Ouch," Annie cried.

Mary rubbed her backside as she stood. "Sorry about that, Sis. I got a bit carried away."

Annie grimaced as she ran her hand up and down

the arm she'd landed on. "I'm going to have bruises here."

"Sorry!" Mary said, kissing her on the cheek.

"No worries. Okay, so this is the place. You can reserve it for your date with no problem, right?"

"Yep. And Rebecca said we could have the reception at Black Eyed Pea."

Annie opened and closed her mouth suddenly. "Black Eyed Pea?"

Mary nodded. "Yes, isn't that fantastic?"

Annie started to head toward the front door, with her head hanging low.

Mary caught up to her and bounced in front of her. "You're not angry about that, are you, Sis?"

Annie raised her chin and blinked. "I guess I just thought you'd have it at Sweet Magnolia."

Mary reached out and placed her hands on Annie's arms. "I love Sweet Magnolia, Annie, but it's your special place with Jack. We can have family parties there, birthday celebrations, and even baby showers, but I want to preserve your memories of your beautiful day. Let me pick where I want my special memories made, okay?"

Annie's eyes began to mist. "You're absolutely right. This is your day and your memories. Black Eyed Pea will be a great place. Besides, Grandmother and Auntie love

Rebecca's grandmother so much. They'll have a blast. Let's just not let them have too many Bloody Marys. Rebecca's grandmother can make some pretty potent ones."

The two women walked out of the church, holding hands. They casually turned and gave the old little white clapboard building one last look. "Maybe we can also add some greenery out here to spruce the porch up." Annie winked at Mary.

"You got it, Sis. We'll decorate this little house of worship, and it'll be the best little wedding chapel in all of Charleston."

CHAPTER TWELVE

"Can you believe Ashton turns one this month?" Annie pulled out the cold cuts to make sandwiches.

"Are we going to have a full-blown party, complete with jumping castle and clowns?"

Annie whirled around and stared at him, waiting for the serious look plastered on his face to crack. He held his stare, not wavering an inch.

"Jumping castle and clowns?" She started to slather salad dressing on the slices of bread.

"He's our firstborn." He came up behind her and circled his arms around her.

"Yes, but that might just be a tad over-the-top." She placed some lunch meat and then cheese on the bread slices.

"I want two slices," he said, peering over her shoulder.

She slapped a second piece on. "I do think we should have the family over at least."

"Sounds great ... that's all he needs," he teased, before grabbing a sandwich off the plate and taking a bite.

"HAPPY BIRTHDAY, DEAR ASHTON, HAPPY BIRTHDAY TO you," the group sang.

Ashton picked up his cupcake, made especially for his birthday, and opened wide. Annie clicked away with the camera feature on her phone as he devoured the little cake, smearing chocolate ear to ear. He giggled as he stuck his tongue out and licked more of the gooey icing.

"Look." Jack pointed. "He even got some in his hair."

Sighing, Annie shook her head. "He'll need a real dunking in the bath tonight." A smile lit up her face as she watched on.

Ashton raised his arms above his head. "Me done," he said.

Annie, armed with a dozen sheets of wet paper towels, went to work on cleaning up his face.

Ashton bounced up and down, trying to avoid the wet cloths. He pointed to the huge red and yellow jumping castle. "Go," he said.

Jack took his little hand and the two made their way over to the castle. He gingerly set him inside and then climbed in after.

"Seems a little overkill with the jumping castle, Sis," Mary whispered into her ear.

Annie stood watching Jack jump with Ashton. "I know, but Jack insisted."

"Grandmother and Auntie are having a ball with the clown, though." Mary smirked at Annie. The two grabbed at their sides and almost fell over from laughing so hard.

"I just wanted a picture of Ashton with chocolate all over his face, while he devoured his birthday cupcake." Annie snapped pictures of Jack and Ashton laughing inside the jumping castle. Their giggles could be heard a mile away.

After Jack got his reconnecting with his inner-child out of his system by playing in the jumping castle, he held Ashton's hand while the clown blew up balloons and twisted them into funny shapes. Aunt Mary painted his little face with butterflies and lady bugs, and when it came time to open presents, it wasn't just Jack who went overboard.

Boxes piled to her chin, Annie struggled with the door to bring them inside. Jack held the door open for her. "Looks like Christmas," he said, laughing.

Annie cut him a stern look. "Exactly what I didn't want. He's one. He doesn't need all of this stuff."

"Aw, come on, Annie. He's only going to be one, once." He leaned over and took the top few boxes from her and headed down to Ashton's bedroom.

"I just wanted a picture of him with chocolate smeared all over his face," she yelled out, getting the last word.

Jack belted out a hardy laugh. "Okay, next year, just the jumping castle."

Annie took a lightweight box and tossed it at him. "Jack Powell, you're absolutely incorrigible. You and Ashton are going to drive me crazy. I can see it now." She couldn't keep the stern look going for long and broke into a wide smile.

"You know you love us," Jack said, making his way back from the bedroom and taking the rest of the packages. He leaned forward and kissed her.

"I love you both more than I could have ever imagined was possible."

"Let's get back out there and rescue the clown from Lilly and Patty," Jack said grinning.

Annie giggled. "The last time I looked over there, it

was your mom asking him to make her a dog out of balloons."

Jack knitted his brows. "Well at least she didn't get in the jumping castle. I was waiting for that." A scowl formed and then he broke into laughter.

The two headed back out to the gathering. Annie squeezed in between Mary and Ashton at the picnic bench. She grabbed one of the bubble wands and dipped it in the tray blowing a string of bubbles out into the breeze. Ashton giggled non stop as he tried to emulate her.

Now that Ashton's birthday party was over with, the preparations for Mary's wedding continued. But even Annie required some downtime.

The news traveled fast and no one could be happier for Vicky and Scott when their adoption finalized then Annie and Jack. Vicky and Scott were now the parents of a darling two-year-old little girl named Jasmine. The two women found playdates a good thing to help, not only burn off some energy for their toddlers, but a time to get together and talk about marriage, children, and life. Days at the beach were especially nice, and since they lived within walking distance to a very quiet and private beach, the foursome headed there on many days.

Annie would pile her car with the special beach wagon Jack had made that easily slid along the sand, as well as buckets, shovels, and other sand toys, a couple of lawn chairs, and of course an umbrella. She also had her large beach bag packed with sunscreen, sun hats, and towels. Vicky packed the cooler with water, juice, and snacks.

They pulled up to Vicky and Scott's house and parked the car. Annie began to unload the back of the van when Vicky came out onto the porch. "Good morning, Annie," she called as she shielded her eyes from the already intense sun and heat. Summertime heat in Charleston could be a bit oppressive.

"Hey, there, are you guys ready?"

"We are."

Annie removed the beach wagon and loaded it up with their stuff and she and Ashton waited for them.

Vicky came out, pulling the cooler by the handle with one hand, and holding Jasmine's little hand with her other.

"Oh, my goodness, she looks so cute in her little pink cover-up and matching water shoes. And the sunglasses! She's really rocking those. I got a pair of sunglasses for

Ashton, too. But he keeps pulling them off and throwing them." Annie laughed.

"He's going to be a ballplayer, that one is," Vicky said, nodding toward Ashton as he reached for a rock on the ground.

"Ashton," Annie yelled, pulling the rock out of his hand. "No, leave it there." She grabbed his hand, and they all proceeded to walk down the pathway behind Vicky and Scott's house that led to the beach. It was a quick walk, thank goodness. Annie's arms were tired just from pulling the wagon and holding on to Ashton's hand.

The women spread blankets and set up the umbrella, and then slathered the sunscreen on each of the kids first, and then themselves.

"Me thirsty," Ashton said, pointing to the cooler.

"And, so now it starts," Annie said, grinning. She reached inside and produced a juice box. She popped the straw in place and handed it to him. He started to take off with the drink in his hand. "No, sit here and drink it," Annie said, giving him *the look*.

After he finished his drink, the women took the kids down near the water. They sat in the wet sand and watched as the kids dug in the sand and soon began trying to eat some, and also throw some.

Annie sighed. "Kids."

"This is all new to me," Vicky said, watching Jasmine play nicely.

"Girls are different than boys. Look at her. She's just so darling, playing so nicely. Then there is Ashton throwing globs of wet sand." She shook her head.

"She's very quiet," Vicky whispered, scooching closer to Annie. "I'm a little worried about her speech. She says very little."

"Do you think she hears okay?" Annie asked with a concerned look on her face.

"She's been to the pediatrician. It seems like everything is okay. There just might be a slight delay in her speech. I hope it's more because of her shyness and not anything medical."

Annie reached out and stroked her friend's arm. "I'm sure it's nothing to worry about. She's precious. I know you said she came from a teenage mom. How long was she in the system before you all were able to adopt her?"

"Since she was a few days old. She's been in a foster home for most of her life. I know she bonded with her foster family. I think this will take time for her to feel as comfortable with us as she felt with them."

"I know, but you and Scott are wonderful folks. You'll give her space and the love she needs. She'll come around. I just know it."

"Her foster family was African American. The

agency didn't say it, but I got the impression they'd rather have placed her with a black family. I hope she'll feel as comfortable with us in time."

"Don't give that another thought. She'll love you guys like you're her biological parents, and it won't matter that she's a little browner than you. She has the loveliest skin tone."

"I don't know which parent was black or which one was white. And it doesn't matter to us."

"And nor should it. She's a sweet little girl."

"I'm learning how to care for her hair. It's been an experience." Vicky lifted her curls and bounced them in the palm of her hand.

"Her little ponytails are cute. You're doing a great job." Annie tilted her head and with one hand, held her floppy hat in place and looked up. "It's a beautiful day."

"It's going to be hotter than you know what, later. One hundred degrees I heard," Vicky said, brushing sand off of Jasmine's face.

"We should be getting the kids back to the air conditioning soon. Let's let them dip their feet in the water one last time, shall we?" Annie grabbed Ashton by the hand. "Let's go put our toes in the water, Ashton," she said, pulling him along.

Vicky and Jasmine followed them, and for a few minutes, they walked along the edge of the cold water.

Annie washed the sand off of Ashton's butt and legs. He sat down in the water, and a wave came up, almost knocking him over. Annie quickly picked him up before he swallowed any water. "More," he said.

Annie shook her head. "This boy is crazy." She let him sit back down and soon another wave came. Annie held him up so he wouldn't wash away. He laughed as he played in the water. "And Mary thinks Ashton is going to be the ring bearer at her wedding. Can you see that going down smoothly?"

"Is Crystal going to be the flower girl?"

Annie nodded. "She'll be okay. It's this little guy that I'm worried about. He'll probably toss the ring into the pews."

Vicky laughed.

Although Ashton wailed and stomped his feet, the two women gathered up all the toys and items they'd brought and headed back to the house. Annie knew that as soon as she bathed him, he'd take a nice long nap.

"Thanks again for the lovely playdate. I don't know if I get more out of it or if the kids do," Annie said, shaking her head at Ashton.

"We need to get the guys together soon, too. Scott's been mentioning a barbecue."

"That sounds great. I could get into some of your delicious margaritas."

"You got it. By the way, we didn't talk about them, but have you hooked up with our college sisters at all?" Vicky asked, now holding Jasmine who was rubbing her eyes.

Annie raised her head and smiled, then reached out and brushed Jasmine's cheek with her fingers. "Someone is tired. No, I haven't heard from them. I saw Jessica at the grocery store with Reece. He's getting to be such a big boy. I think he's four years old or maybe even a little older. She promises to get together soon, but it never happens. I'm just as much at fault."

Vicky nodded. "I got a call from Cassie about three months ago. I told her all about the adoption and how I was praying it would go through. I thought maybe she'd follow up on it, but so far nothing."

"Before this summer is over with, we have to get together with them." Annie paused before she breathed in a large amount of humid air. "I know. That barbecue you were talking about ... what if we invited them, too?"

Vicky nodded and shrugged her shoulders. "If you think they'll come."

"If they don't, then we'll know we've outgrown one another. I know life gets busy and time slips through our fingers, but if we don't set aside some time or make time for our friendships, then they will disintegrate like burning paper, blowing in the breeze."

"Wow, that's pretty deep. I could totally see your burning paper image," Vicky said, tipping her chin up and down.

Annie laughed. "You plan the barbecue, and I'll send out the invites."

"You sure you don't want to have it over at Sweet Magnolia? It's such a beautiful property. We don't have much of a backyard here, since we're right up against the dunes. I mean, I guess we could have a beach party?"

"We can have it at our place. I tell you what, I know Scott's wanted to try out the new gas grill he got. He's told Jack as much. Let's get together over here, just us, and we can plan the big party to have at my place. How does that sound?" Annie quirked a brow as she waited for Vicky's answer.

Vicky switched Jasmine to her other hip. "Perfect. We'll be in touch. But right now, I'm going to get this little angel out of this heat. Are you sure you don't want to come in for some iced tea?" She took a step toward the front door.

"Nope, this guy is getting rinsed off and a nap. Thank you, though." Annie opened the car doors to let some of the heat out, and then started the engine. She turned the air conditioning on high to get the cool air started, and then strapped Ashton into his car seat. By the time they drove up to Sweet Magnolia, a whole three minutes later, Ashton had already fallen fast asleep.

Annie huffed and puffed as she carried Ashton and the beach bag up the stairs. She pushed open the front door, where she was immediately greeted by Isla and Buffy.

She dropped the beach bag on the floor and proceeded to the bathroom, where she drew a bath for Ashton with tepid water. She stripped him out of his wet and sandy beach clothes and placed him into the bath. She splashed some water on him and took the bar of soap to his skin. She quickly rinsed off the soapy water and wrapped him in a towel. Putting a loose fitting outfit on him, she laid him in his crib. He didn't argue a single bit. "I know, that's right, sleep, you're a tired boy."

She started to head out of the room when he called out. "Water, Mommy."

She stopped and sighed. "Okay, I'll be right back."

She entered the kitchen and filled up his sippy cup with water. She felt a bit dizzy but pushed through and gave him his water. He took two sips, then fell back down on the mattress and closed his eyes.

After placing his cup on the dresser nearby, the room began to spin. Feeling faint, she grabbed onto the doorjamb and scooted along the wall, down the hall toward their bedroom. She made it to the bed and plopped down. She breathed heavily for a moment and could feel her heart racing a mile a minute. *What on earth was happening*? She took a couple of deep breaths and tried to steady her racing pulse. She leaned back against the pillows and pulled her legs up onto the mattress. She closed her eyes for a moment and doesn't remember the rest.

CHAPTER THIRTEEN

J ack took the damp washcloth to the bathroom sink and wet it with more cool water. He caught a glimpse of his worried expression in the mirror. He continued to ring out the cloth, and then taking a deep breath for strength, entered the bedroom where Annie rested.

Annie tried to smile to let Jack know she was feeling better. "Thanks, babe." She reached over and placed her hand on top of his.

"You gave me a scare. I'm glad I got off early and came home."

"I'm glad, too," she whispered.

"I have Ashton in the playpen. Let me go get him."

Annie pulled her body up into a sitting position. Her mouth was parched and she looked for a glass of water.

There, on the nightstand, she spotted a glass filled to the brim with refreshing water. She sipped it slowly at first, and then took a couple of gulps.

"Hey, hey, slow down there," Jack said, plopping down onto the bed next to her, while holding Ashton. Ashton wiggled out of his arms and soon snuggled his mom's neck.

Annie wrapped her arms around him and breathed in his warm scent from the bath products she'd used on him earlier, holding him tightly.

"How are you feeling?" Jack locked his eyes on her, while he waited for her answer, holding his breath just a little.

"I feel a little weak. I guess I got dehydrated today."

"I think so. I called Vicky to see how you felt today while at the beach. She said she thought you were okay, but it was hot out, and she couldn't recall you drinking any water."

"Yeah, I made sure Ashton got juice, but I forgot about myself. It was rather warm outside. I came in and washed the sand off of him and put him down for a nap. I felt a bit lightheaded, so I came in here. That's the last I remember."

"Well, I called Michael, just to run your symptoms by him. He said to keep an eye on you, and if your symptoms worsen, I'm to bring you right in."

Annie shook her head. "No, really, I'm feeling pretty good. I just need a bit more fluids in me." She reached for the glass again.

"He's going to stop by when he gets off his shift." Jack looked down at his watch. "He should be here soon."

Annie furrowed her brows. "Michael? He's coming to make a house call?" Annie snuggled with Ashton while she waited.

Isla and Buffy barked. "I think he may be here, now." Jack moved from the bed to the doorway. "Stay in bed," he said, shaking his finger.

Annie could hear the men talking in the other room. Her face turned red when Michael walked into the room and greeted her. "I feel so dumb. I know the dangers of heat and not drinking enough water. I should have been drowning in water. Well, not literally, but you know what I mean," Annie said, pulling her twisted mouth to the right.

"It's an easy mistake to make. Unfortunately, it can be a deadly one, as well," Michael said, taking out his stethoscope. "Let me take a listen." He leaned over.

"Jack," Annie said, motioning him to take Ashton.

"Your heart sounds pretty good. Your pulse is still a bit slow, but not critical. Get some more fluids in you, rest in bed for a bit longer, and I think you'll be good as new."

"Thanks, Michael, for coming over. This is beyond the call of duty," Jack said, placing his hand on Michael's shoulder.

"Hey, that's what friends are for."

"By the way, how's Rebecca doing?"

"She's doing great. She's so over the pregnancy, though. She wants the baby out." He laughed.

"I know exactly how she feels. How many more days?" Annie rubbed little Ashton's back, who now snuggled on her lap once again.

Michael looked at his watch. "Let's see ... she's due in four days. They'll induce her if she hasn't had her by the end of the week."

"I can't wait to hold her," Annie said, wrinkling up her nose. "I love babies."

Michael took a few steps toward the door. "You take care of yourself. No more days out on the beach without bottled water. It's easy to sweat out the moisture, while out in the hot sun."

"Got it, Doc. Give my love to Rebecca." Annie watched as the fellows left the room. She scooted down under the covers, while holding Ashton. She wrapped her arms around him even snugger, and kissed his little neck. She'd baby him as long as she could.

CHAPTER FOURTEEN

Annie stumbled into the living room to find Jack and Ashton eating animal crackers on the sofa, with both Isla and Buffy eagerly waiting for crumbs, or if they were lucky, the entire cookies that would slip out of Ashton's tiny grip.

"*Ahem,*" she said, startling the two snackers.

"Hey, babe, how are you feeling? Did you have a nice nap?" Jack patted the seat cushion next to them.

Annie strolled over to the sofa, but not before giving both pups a rub on the head. She plopped down with a loud, "*Ugh.*"

"I see you fixed dinner," she said, eyeing the cookies.

"This is dessert. He had raviolis, green beans, and milk," Jack said, smiling from ear to ear, clearly proud of his accomplishment on dinner detail.

Annie held her hands out to Ashton. He looked at his cookie and quickly stuffed it into his mouth before he flew into her arms. Annie held him back and gazed into his sparkling eyes. "So, you think you're getting away with something, don't you, you little rascal." Annie blew raspberries on his neck and made him laugh.

"Really, honey. He ate a good dinner. I think he deserves these cookies," Jack said coyly. He folded down the bag and stuck the cookies back into the box and sealed it. "But, he's probably had enough," he said, jumping up and moving toward the kitchen.

"More," Ashton yelled as he watched the cookies disappear out of his sight.

"You've had enough," Annie said, pressing her forehead to his.

Jack entered the living room. "Why don't you go take a shower and get comfy? I can entertain this guy some more."

Annie sighed. "I'm kind of hungry." She pulled up from the sofa and put Ashton down on the floor. He toddled around the pups and headed for the kitchen. "I think he's after those darn cookies," she said, shaking her head.

"What do you feel like eating? I can scramble up some eggs, warm up the leftover raviolis, make you a peanut butter—"

"Jack, honey, I appreciate your thoughtfulness, but I'm not dying. I just got a little dehydrated."

Jack hung his head and stared at his bare feet.

"*Tsk*. I'm sorry, I didn't mean to hurt your feelings." Annie quickly stepped toward him and brought him into her hold. "I love how you dote on me, I really do. I guess I'm not used to being the one helped. I'm always the helper. It's a strange role reversal for me." Her eyes never wavered from his.

He kissed her softly, and she nearly melted into him. He stepped back and bushed her hair from her forehead. "You two are the most important people in my life. Let me love you. Let me help you when you need it. I know you'll soon be back in the helper role." He leaned forward and kissed her lips, sending chills up and down her spine.

She began to feel lightheaded again, but this time she knew perfectly well it wasn't from dehydration. It was from being so full of love. "I love you, Jack Powell, and I always will."

～

"SEVEN POUNDS THREE OUNCES. HEAD FULL OF DARK WAVY hair," the voice said on the other side of the phone.

"Rebecca!" Annie screamed into the phone.

Rebecca sighed into the receiver. "She's beautiful, Annie. I can't wait for you to meet her."

"What did you name her?"

"It's kind of old-school, but when your mom's name is Rebecca, and your dad's name is Michael, I guess you got it coming. Kathryn," Rebecca said.

"Kathryn ... oh, I adore that. It's so elegant. I love everything about it," Annie said.

"I know they'll eventually call her Kate, but I'll hold on to Kathryn as long as I can."

"Well, you never dithered from Rebecca, and I've known Michael a long time, and he's never gone by anything but Michael." Annie realized she might have said too much regarding knowing him a long time. She sputtered a bit before continuing. "Well, you know what I mean. I just meant ..."

"It's okay, Annie. I know you and Michael share a past. It's no big deal. You're married to Jack, and I'm married to Michael. Let's be big girls about this."

"You're right, I don't know why I blubbered on so. I'm sorry."

"Anyway, when are you going to come over and see Kathryn?"

～

They waited until Rebecca and Kathryn had a chance to bond before they barraged her with visits. Annie organized the trip, and Grandmother, along with Auntie, Mary, Betsy, and even Morgan, who had stopped in to visit family, showed up bearing gifts.

Each woman took turns holding the new bundle, while Rebecca opened gifts. "You all didn't need to do this. You already gave me a wonderful baby shower," she said, holding up the cutest dress ever in purple, with matching bloomers.

"I know, but these are her coming home gifts," Grandmother said boldly.

Rebecca tipped her head toward Grandmother Lilly. "Thank you, ma'am."

"It's our pleasure, dear," Patty said, lifting her chin and then settling her eyes on Kathryn once again.

"We don't want to wear you out, or our welcome, so we'll be going now," Annie said, pulling up from the comfy chair.

"When do you think we can talk about the reception?" Mary said.

Annie cut a look at Mary, making her lower her head. "Not now, Mary," she said through clenched teeth.

"Give me another week or so, and we'll get together. I'll call you."

Mary lifted her head and nodded. "Okay, when

you're ready. We still have plenty of time, it's still only August."

"When is your date again?"

"October tenth."

"Okay, we do have time. I've already given Grand-mother a heads-up about it. I'll check in with her, and we'll get something together to present to you."

"Sounds great, Rebecca," Annie and Mary said at the same time.

Annie playfully bumped shoulders with Mary, then laughed. "In the meantime, we can discuss decorations for the church." Annie put her arm around Mary and pulled her in for a hug.

Mary nodded. "Sounds good."

"Okay, well, we're off. Have a great day. Love this little girl with all your might. She's a beauty. I bet Michael is just beside himself," Annie said.

Rebecca sighed. "He loves her, that's for sure, but his schedule is so crazy. I had no idea being married to a doctor would be so lonely sometimes."

Annie brushed her hand up Rebecca's arm and held it there. "Anytime you need to talk, I'm here." She leaned in and kissed Rebecca on the cheek.

The crew got back into the van and headed to Grandmother's first to drop off her, Auntie, and Betsy. Once there, Morgan said she'd walk the rest of the way.

"Kathryn is such a baby doll," Mary said, shaking her head.

"Just beautiful," Annie said, echoing Mary's sentiment.

"I'm surprised she hadn't thought of Michael's career being so involved before now, aren't you?" Mary asked.

Annie raised her brow. "Sort of, but I guess when you're in love, you don't think about those things."

"I'm sure they'll find their happy place and work it all out." Mary grabbed her vibrating phone. "Hello?"

Annie couldn't help but overhear. It obviously was Danny on the phone. Mary whispered, but she could tell by the tone of her voice that it was a conversation between two lovers.

"Danny." Mary said, putting her phone back into her pocket.

"I figured it was," Annie said, winking.

"I got the invitations, and I'll be sending those out soon. When can we talk decorations?"

"Come over, anytime. I have a few ideas, too. I've been saving pictures from Pinterest and other sites in a folder on my laptop," Annie said.

CHAPTER FIFTEEN

A nnie rapped on Vicky and Scott's front door. Jack had Ashton's legs straddling over his shoulders, while holding his hands. They were carrying on laughing, and Jack made a few sudden moves as if he were going to drop Ashton, making Ashton laugh even harder. Annie reached up and pulled down the back of Ashton's shirt that had ridden up, showing off his colorful diaper.

"Hey, you guys," Vicky said, opening the door for them to enter. "Glad you could make it." She stepped back and let them pass her before she closed the door. "Jack, Scott is out on the back deck," she said as she patted Ashton on the back. "Jasmine is playing on the floor with her blocks. Do you want to play, too?"

Ashton nodded. Jack gently set Ashton down on his

two feet and watched as he toddled off to find Jasmine. They were fast becoming friends.

"Come on, Annie, I could use your help in the kitchen."

The two ladies headed into the kitchen while Jack made his way onto the deck. From the kitchen, they had a clear view into the living room, where they could keep a careful watch over the children.

"Pull up a stool," Vicky said, nodding toward the black wrought iron swivel stools.

"Thought you needed help?" Annie crossed her hands at her chest.

"That's code word for gossip!" Vicky tossed her head back and laughed. Annie joined in. Soon the kids in the room were belting out laughs, imitating them, which made them laugh some more. "They're at the age of monkey see, monkey do."

Vicky opened the fridge and pulled out a glass pitcher. Annie's eyes widened when she saw the lime colored concoction. "Yes, please," Annie said, nodding her head several times. "It's a margarita kind of day," she added, putting her elbows up on the counter and cradling her face.

"Aw, what's going on?" Vicky asked as she poured two glasses.

"Just life. I'm trying to help Mary plan her wedding.

I'm trying to let go of the business, and ..." She sighed and didn't bother finishing her sentence.

"It's what you want to do, right? Because life's too short to be doing stuff you don't want to do."

Annie took a short sip of her drink. "Yes, I want to help Mary, for sure, and I think I do want to give up some control at the cupcakery. I want to spend more time with Ashton, and well, we're talking about expanding our family." She took another sip. "This is very good."

"Thanks. It's going to be an easy dinner, just some grilled burgers and hotdogs, potato salad, and beans. I hope that's okay?"

Annie nodded. "It sounds delicious. Simple is good. How's Jasmine doing?" Annie whispered.

"She's coming around. She still has moments of shyness, anxiety, and insecurity, but we just wrap our arms around her when she's having a little meltdown, and then we redirect her. She is a good sweet kid." Vicky looked over Annie's shoulder and studied the children playing.

"Ashton has a few of those meltdowns, too. It could be because he's just plain spoiled." Annie smirked.

"It's easy to spoil the first one. Wait until you do have your second. Ashton will act out for other reasons, and you'll have to deal with that."

Annie stared off into space for a moment, recalling when her parents had brought Mary home from the hospital. There was a big age difference between them, and she had to think back if she had been jealous at all of the new baby. "*Hmm*, you're right. It can be a bit tricky when you bring a new baby home. I better start thinking about how to handle that." She laughed.

"Are you pregnant?" Vicky's eyes widened.

"No, not yet, but we are trying." Annie curled up her lips at the corner and then sipped her drink. "You don't think I'd be indulging in alcohol, if I was pregnant, do you?"

Vicky tightened her lips. "No, but thank you for reminding me. I'll know the signs to look for now, for when you are." She playfully tapped Annie's hand.

"Ha ha." Annie raised her glass to Vicky. "To friendship."

Vicky clinked her glass with Annie's. "To friendship," she repeated. "Speaking of friendships, what are we going to do to get the old gang together?" She pulled up a stool and sat down.

The women chatted, and now and then, they could hear shrills coming from the living room and some boisterous laughter coming from the deck. They soon had a workable plan for a future get-together, and both Annie and Vicky were satisfied their plan would be a success. They were both very determined.

Their concentration broke when the guys entered the kitchen. "Hey, we're hungry," Scott announced in a very loud voice.

Vicky and Annie slid off their stools. "We're ready. We were just waiting on y'all," Annie said.

Vicky handed Scott the plate of perfectly round hamburger patties and a couple of hot dogs. She handed Jack a clean plate to put the cooked food on. The two guys headed back outside, but not before grabbing a couple of longnecks out of the fridge.

Annie watched them as they weaved their way around the blocks, cars, and kids. Jack reached down and patted Ashton on the head before going outside. "Jack is the best dad ever," Annie said, smiling.

"Scott's not too bad at the job, himself," Vicky chimed in.

"Of course, he is. I always knew you'd be great parents."

"I know, I'm just proud of how he's taken on the role of father so well," Vicky said as she looked lovingly on toward the children playing in the other room.

Annie wrapped her arm around her friend's shoulders and squeezed her. "And you're a great mother, too."

"Okay, put those chairs over there," Annie said, motioning toward the shade trees. "And then, move the round table in between them," she added.

Vicky began covering the tables with red and white checkered table cloths, while Scott and Jack finished stringing the little white lights through the trees and above the sitting areas.

Annie began to lug some wood from the pile and stack it inside the fire pit. She brought a few extra to put on the side. She stood back with her hands on her hips and admired how they'd transformed the property into a festive party place.

"Tonight, with the lights on and the fire going, it's going to be so magical," Vicky said, coming to stand next to Annie.

"Yup, I'm so happy this is going to happen finally. How long has it been?"

"Too long, but we won't harp on that too much or they won't ever come back." Vicky playfully knocked shoulders with Annie.

"True." She looked down at her wrist. "We have about forty-five more minutes before Milly brings the kids back."

"It was so nice of her to offer to watch Jasmine, too."

"She loves kids. And besides, Ashton is growing sweet on little Jasmine."

~

"How do I look?" Annie twirled around.

"Beautiful," Jack said wrapping his arms around her waist and pulling her in for a hug.

"You say that all the time." She leaned in and kissed his lips.

"I say it all the time because it's true." He made her blush with his sweet words. She moved her hands up his back and held him close. "I love you," Jack said.

"I love you, too."

Jack held her back a few inches and knitted his brows while studying her face. "What? Why are you just looking at me?"

"Nothing. I'm just trying to run it all through my mind right now."

"Run what through your mind right now?" he asked.

"How we met ... the first time I knew I was falling in love with you." She smiled at him.

"I knew almost the first moment we met that you were special, and I was determined to see where it went. I was hoping for this, but you just never know." Jack's eyes narrowed.

"Me, too. Remember the boat ride and the night we got caught in the downpour?"

Jack tipped his head. "Yes, that was the night for sure that I knew I wouldn't let you go without a fight. I hope tonight goes the way you and Vicky want it to, but remember one thing for me, okay?" Jack pulled her arms off his back and held her hands in his.

Annie pulled her bottom lip between her teeth and waited.

"You and Ashton are the most important people in my life, and always will be. Men see friendships a bit differently than women. I am more invested in the friendships we make as a couple, than hanging out with my old college buddies and drinking ourselves under the table. But, I get it, you, Vicky, Cassie, and Jessica had a bond that was important to you. And I bet you'll find they haven't forgotten you so much, as it's just been about life getting in the way. They probably are working long hours. We know they have children, and then, you know, we husbands do need a lot of attention, too." He winked at her.

Annie melted into Jack's arms. A few tears escaped her lids, and she quickly wiped them away. She pushed back slightly, and stared into his big eyes. "I love you. I can't say it enough. You know me so well. It's true, I have these expectations, and partly it's because I don't want to let go of that part of my life, but at the same time, I love my new life, and well, I guess I want it all," she said in total adoration.

Jack pushed her hair back away from her face and left his hand on her cheek. She moved her hand up and cupped his hand. "I know, that's exactly my point. And maybe this will be the night that Cassie and Jessica will come back into your life on a more regular basis. If you all want this, you have to make it happen." He leaned in and kissed her hand, then moved to her mouth. Annie relaxed her shoulders, dropping her gaze. Jack lifted her chin with his finger. "Now, go finish getting ready. They'll be arriving soon. I'll start getting the food out."

Annie headed toward the bathroom to freshen up. While in there, she heard Vicky and Scott arrive. She stood tall while she brushed her hair, smiling as she did.

Annie bounced down the hall in her baby blue sundress and white sandals. "Vicky, Scott, Jasmine," she said, leaning down and kissing Jasmine on the cheek.

"It's party time," Vicky bellowed.

"I hear cars coming," Annie said, her eyes widening to the size of saucers.

"It's going to be okay. These are your friends who you've known forever. Take a deep breath," Jack said with both hands squarely on her shoulders as he looked deeply into her eyes.

Annie nodded. Then they heard car doors shut and soon a knock on the door. Annie rushed to the front door and opened it wide. There stood Cassie, Ryan, and their five-year-old daughter Katy. Annie warmly smiled at the group and then held out her arms. Cassie ran into them, and after a few happy tears, Jessica, Tom, and their now four-year-old son Reece also showed up.

Once all the hugs and handshakes were shared, the group headed outside. The men took the kids and walked down to the dock to give the ladies a little bit of alone time. *Who said men didn't have feelings?*

"Vicky made the sangria. Isn't it delicious?" Annie said, topping off Cassie's and Jessica's glasses.

When the men returned, they found the women a bit giddy, laughing and hugging, and they even witnessed a few tears. They weren't about to get in the middle of that.

Before Annie realized it, Jack and Scott had grilled the pre-cooked ribs, brought out all the sides, and everyone was digging into the delicious food.

The group watched from lawn chairs as Jack built a huge fire. Light from the full moon shone brightly, and along with the brilliant flames reaching up as if to shake hands with the moon, the area remained well lit.

Jack didn't really know Cassie's or Jessica's husbands, but men did what men did best, and they talked about sports, boats, race cars, and when talk of conflict came up, Scott had a few war stories to share. It brought the reality home for Jack about what Danny had been through.

Jack leaned back in his chair and listened on. He smiled when heard the girls professing their love for each other and promised never to let this much time pass between getting together again.

"I'm so sorry, Annie, if we hurt your feelings. It's so hard trying to make time for a bubble bath, let alone getting together with friends. I haven't had a pedicure in four weeks because I can't make the time for myself," Cassie said, looking down at the chipped paint on her toes.

"I hear you, Cassie. By the time I get off of work and pick up Reece from daycare, it's all I can do to fix dinner before dropping into bed." She pulled her bottom lip out and pouted.

"We all lead extremely busy lives, I know that. And now that Vicky lives so close, we've been able to hang out more, but we just want to see you guys more often," Annie said with half-closed lids. "Can we make a pact right here and now?"

Cassie reached her hand to Vicky. Vicky reached her hand to Jessica, and Annie closed the circle by taking Jessica's and Cassie's hands. "Remember when we pinky swore that we'd be in each other's weddings?"

All the ladies nodded and some made sounds agreeing that they remembered.

"Let's pinky swear we'll do our best to see each other at least every three months."

"I think that's doable," Vicky said, encouraging the group to accept these terms.

Scott leaned over and tapped Jack on the arm. "So, I think this is where the group hug will come in and the waterworks will start."

Jack sighed. "You gotta love these women, right?"

"Okay, so it is September already. Let's plan on seeing each other during Christmas." Annie raised her hand in opposition to any static regarding the holiday chaos. "I know it's a busy time of year, but we can meet anywhere—downtown at a restaurant, coffee shop, a movie, anything."

"Wait! We'll get to see each other next month for Mary's wedding," Vicky interjected.

"That's right. You all are coming, aren't you?" Annie looked at Cassie then at Jessica.

"Yes, we RSVP'd Mary. Didn't she tell you?" Cassie said.

Annie shook her head. "See? Even family can get too busy and forget to share some very important details to the person who is helping with her wedding." Annie scowled.

Everyone laughed.

"Now, come here, y'all." Annie held out her arms, and everyone joined in a big hug.

Scott looked over at Jack and smirked. Then the women started hugging each other individually and crying, or more like sobbing. Scott winked at Jack. He then palm slapped his chest. "Do I know these women or what?"

"Major Scott Collins," Jack said in a deep voice.

Scott perked up and raised his chin and then saluted. "Reporting for wife comforting duty." The two men laughed and then Tom and Ryan raised their bottles, and Scott and Jack followed suit.

Jasmine and Ashton bounced on their daddy's knees as they laughed along. They had no clue how entertaining or funny they were, but all was good at Sweet Magnolia. Jasmine leaned over and hugged Ashton.

Annie caught a glimpse of the male bonding that was happening on the other side of the firepit, and just as she was turning back to the women, she saw Jasmine hug Ashton. "Look, Vicky," Annie said, tugging at her arm.

"I hope they grow up to be best friends and always

find time for one another," Vicky said, slurring her words some.

Annie figured the wine talked for them all that night, but she didn't care. She was happy that their rekindling of friendship finally happened and it brought her so much joy.

ANNIE WATCHED AS THE LAST SET OF TAILLIGHTS DROVE out of view. She wrapped her arms around Jack and waited for his kiss.

"I hope everyone gets home safely," she said, snuggling into his neck.

"Both Ryan and Tom had stopped drinking," Jack said, leading her into the house.

"You were monitoring their drinking?" Annie said.

"Yep, Scott and I. We're responsible like that," he said, grinning.

They pushed open the door to Ashton's bedroom and peeked in. With their arms wrapped around each other, they stared at him, watching as his chest rose and fell. Satisfied, they tiptoed out of Ashton's room and pulled the door closed.

Jack grabbed her hands in his and leaned in for a

kiss. "We all talked about it before you women got wasted."

"Wasted! We were not," Annie put her hands on her hips. "A little tipsy, perhaps, but more like relaxed," she said, tipping her forehead to Jack.

Jack pulled her in close and studied her face. "We just knew that this would be a very emotional night and we wanted to be available to you, if you needed us." He rocked her back and forth in his arms.

"Uh huh, emotionally available," Annie repeated.

"Absolutely." He let out a low belly laugh, unable to contain the bantering or game playing any longer.

Annie leaned in and kissed his warm mouth. When he felt her start to pull away, he held her in place and kissed her passionately. She parted her lips and welcomed him in. He ran his hand up the back of her neck and pushed his fingers through her hair. She moaned softly. She reached for his arms and ran her hands up his bulging muscles, then cupping his face, she leaned into him hard. He suddenly broke loose and grabbed her by the hand, leading them toward their bedroom. Once inside, he gently laid her down on their king-size bed. She pulled her bottom lip in and gazed lovingly at her husband as he pulled his tee shirt over his head, revealing his chiseled chest. She scooted up toward the middle of the bed and opened her arms for him, her heart pounding a mile a minute. "I love you, Jack," she said, pulling him in. He trailed kisses up and down her neck before finding her mouth. But just before he kissed her, he lovingly studied her face. "You make me so happy. I love you, Annie Powell." Then he took hungry possession of her mouth with deep sweeping strokes of his tongue. She cradled his head in her hands and deepened the kiss.

CHAPTER SIXTEEN

Mary met with Annie four more times during a ten-day stretch to go over last-minute details. *Talk about a bridezilla.*

"You confirmed the delivery of the flowers, right, Mary?"

Mary read the list of checked items on her phone. "Yup."

"Okay, and we, of course, got the limo. Robert and Milly were super cool about lending a car to us."

"And Diane was so thoughtful about hooking us up with this cute beach bungalow on Folly Beach for three nights."

"Okay, let's talk about Crystal and Ashton."

Mary tightened her lips and nodded. "I see Crystal

pulling a flowered covered wagon with Ashton sitting inside. He'll carry the ring on a pillow. Crystal will toss petals the best she can, but her role will be to make sure the wagon makes its way to us and that Ashton doesn't fall out."

"I think the ring should be in a box. I can just see Ashton now ... he'll either lose the ring or throw it out on purpose." Annie twisted her mouth like a pretzel as she played out either of these scenarios in her head.

"Okay, can Jack make us a small box at his shop?" Mary quirked a brow and tilted her head.

"I'll ask, but it shouldn't be a problem," Annie said, jotting down notes. "Now, for sure, Danny's parents are going to be there, right?"

Mary shrugged. "As far as I know. They haven't RSVP'd yet, but Danny insists they are coming."

"What's their deal, anyway? They're not like Robert and Milly at all," Annie said, pulling back her chair and curling one leg under her bottom.

"I wish Robert and Milly were his folks. I don't know that much about them. They've been over to Milly's a couple of times, but more times than not, they don't accept their invitations."

"Yeah, I know. Jack and I have spoken about it before. He said his aunt and uncle have always been a bit estranged from the main family. He said they always made an excuse as to why they couldn't come to a family event. After a while, they just joked about it."

"Well, the few times I've had the pleasure of their company," Mary said in exaggeration, "I found his mom to be quite, well, how do I say it...?"

"On air?" Annie blurted.

"Uppity," Mary concluded, echoing her sister's sentiment.

"Preston, his dad, seems quiet," Annie said, reaching for the pen to jot something else down.

"Yeah, he is. Susan is the one that thinks her shi—"

"Mary!" Annie said, scowling at her. "That's not very nice."

Mary lifted her left and then her right shoulder up and down and smirked. "Well, it's true."

Annie pulled her leg out from under her and stood. "Coffee?" She made her way into the kitchen.

"How about a glass of wine?"

Annie poured Mary a glass of wine and made herself a cup of coffee. "Okay, so I think we've ironed out all the details. Jack and I are going to show up at the church and receive the flowers and get that all situated. We're going the day before to decorate the inside and the porch. The car is reserved to take you to Black Eyed Pea."

"Yes, and Rebecca and I have agreed on all the food

items," Mary said, perking up now that they were talking about food.

"Betsy is making the cake," Annie added. "Who is transporting the cake to the restaurant?"

Mary's jaw dropped. "Oops, that's one big detail we forgot."

"I can ask Peter to help. He's always up for being a good samaritan." The last time she'd stepped foot into Sweet Indulgence, she'd felt like a stranger in her place of business.

BETSY ASKED ANNIE TO MEET HER AT THE BAKERY. IT seemed odd, but she decided it must have to do with Mary's cake, so she went. She hung up her sweater on the coatrack and then crossed over to the counter.

"Don't mind me, I'm just here as a customer," Annie said, peering into the back where she saw Peter busy at work icing cupcakes.

Peter looked up when he heard Annie's voice. "Hey there, boss. What brings you in here?" He stepped out of the kitchen, wiping his hands on his apron.

"I'm meeting Betsy here," Annie said, nodding. "How is everything?"

"Good. I'm just getting ready to put in the new flavor of the month. I bet you can't guess what it is."

"*Hmm*, let's see ... pumpkin something. Pumpkin cream cheese?"

Peter shook his head. "Try again."

"Cinnamon streusel?"

"Give up?"

"I guess so," Annie said, her eyes locked on his, waiting to hear.

"Chocolate fudge with Peppermint Pattie icing."

"Wow, that's an interesting combination," Annie said. Annie turned when she heard the door open. Betsy had arrived, and Annie waved.

"Hello, Annie. Peter," Betsy said, nodding to them both.

"Can I get you ladies a cup of coffee?"

"That would be nice, Peter."

Annie took Betsy by the arm and lead her to a table where they both sat down. Annie set her clasped hands on the table and smiled. "What sparked this secret meeting today?" Annie kept her eyes focused on Betsy's.

Betsy hesitated, which caused Annie to stir a bit in her chair.

"Is everything all right with Grandmother and Auntie? I know I don't come over as much as I should be, but with Ashton, and now Mary's wedding ..." she stopped rambling and searched Betsy's face for answers. Betsy rested her eyes on the table. "Betsy!" Annie's breath quickened in anticipation of Betsy's words.

"I think it's time they both moved into the cottage at Sweet Magnolia."

A lump lodged in her throat. Annie swallowed, hearing the gulping sound in her ears. She made a second attempt to swallow before speaking. "What's happened? Did they do something to tick you off? Maybe I can—"

"Annie, stop. It's nothing they did. They are getting up there in years and require more help. They're proud so they don't want to ask, but it's getting harder and harder for them to get around. Charles and I have enjoyed living with them, but I think the time has come that they need family around."

Annie nodded. She knew this day would come eventually. She'd had to know, but then again, Grandmother and Auntie were two of the strongest women she'd ever known. When she looked at them, she didn't see aged women, or worse, feeble old women. She saw two vibrant women who defied the nature of getting older. "I see. Well, Jack built the cottage with them in mind. It was always intended for them, but they weren't ready. They might not be ready now, but I guess I'll cross that bridge when I come to it."

"I think they're ready. One of the biggest fears they have is becoming a burden to you and Mary. Especially to you." Betsy sighed and softened her features.

"Two coffees," Peter said, placing a Styrofoam cup in front of each of the women.

"Thanks," Annie whispered. Heaving her shoulders up and down, she picked up her coffee and blew on it before sipping. "What specific things are happening?"

"They need help with showering, now. And I've even helped them get dressed. I'm noticing a bit more forgetfulness, and also, Patty will cry for no reason."

"I see," Annie said.

Betsy reached across the table and patted Annie's hand. "You've been a wonderful granddaughter and niece to them both. They love you so much, but they realize it's time to be closer to you."

The women drank their coffee in silence for a few moments.

"On a happy note, I'm so tickled about Mary's wedding and am honored to make their cake."

"Yes, thank you so much. Preparations are coming along quite well. Moving Grandmother and Auntie right now is going to add to the stress, but it is what it is. We must do what we must do to help them."

"Charles and I have been looking at homes to buy. We found one we like and would like to put an offer in."

"Of course, Betsy, go ahead. I'll talk to Jack tonight about what we need to do to make the cottage ADA compliant and when he thinks he can get that done. If they have to move in with us, then that's what we'll do."

Betsy gasped. "No! They both told me they don't want that. If they can't move into the cottage, they'll run away."

Annie knitted her brows together. She could picture them both saying something childish like that. "Please? Run away?"

"They know they need help, but they're not ready to be moved into your house. Now, that may eventually happen, but for right now, it's 'over my dead body'," Betsy tried her best to imitate Grandmother.

Both women laughed.

"Okay, got it. They need us, but not that badly." Annie smiled.

❧

"ANNIE! IT'S SO NICE TO SEE YOU, DEAR," AUNTIE PATTY said, tilting her face up for a kiss.

Annie looked toward the kitchen when she heard the tapping of Grandmother's cane. Grandmother stopped halfway into the living room, breathing a bit heavy. "Are you all right, Grandmother?"

"Yes, just takes me a bit longer to get to my chair these days."

Annie watched as she walked a few more steps, stopping once more, and then continuing to her chair.

"We're both not getting around as much as we did," Patty said, then she coughed, covering her mouth with a lace hankie.

"Well, that's what brought me here today." Annie's heart pounded in her chest, and the looks on their faces crushed her. *Maybe she should try another approach, than you're too old to be by yourself.* "Charles and Betsy are purchasing their first house together. Isn't that wonderful?"

"I hope they don't think we are moving into their new house," Grandmother said in a brash tone, making the hair on Annie's arms stand.

"No, nothing like that." *Why was this so hard?* "Grandmother," Annie said, making eye contact with her.

Grandmother raised her left brow and angled her head.

"Auntie," Annie continued, looking quickly away.

"Yes, dear?"

"It's time."

Patty dropped her chin and stared at the floor. Grandmother made a *humph* sound.

"Do you know what I mean?" Annie asked in a soft pitch.

"Yes," Grandmother answered.

"Yes," Patty said right afterward.

"Who'd like tea?" Annie hopped up from the sofa and made her way toward the kitchen.

"Annie," Grandmother said, stopping Annie from moving.

Annie slowly turned toward her. "Yes, Grandmother?"

"What about the house?"

Annie shrugged. "Those are details we'll have to work out." Annie rushed toward the kitchen. She reached out and grabbed the counter with both hands, bracing her body. She couldn't stop the tears.

~

"WHAT'S UP, SIS?"

"It's time."

Mary didn't speak for a moment. Then she cleared her throat. "How'd they take it?"

"They took it just fine. However, they're worried about the house."

More silence came from the other end of the phone.

"I know it means the world to them. It has so much history and has been in the family for generations, but I have my home here with Jack, and I don't want to move there. I want them to move into the cottage, but do we sell the house, even though it's against their wishes? Do we let it sit empty until they're both gone? I just don't know what to do."

"It makes perfect sense for them to move into the cottage. That way you'll be there, and if you need to hire additional help, then you can oversee that as well. Doesn't it suck to be the oldest?"

"Mary, I need your help and encouragement, not your snide remarks."

"I'm sorry, I always say dumb things when I'm scared."

"Scared?"

"You know that day will come, Annie. I don't know if I can bear it."

"Listen, those two women have more time on this earth. They just need a little extra from us. They're not ready to check out yet."

"I guess Danny and I could move into the house, instead. The cottage always was intended for them and they need it more than we do. This way, we can keep the maintenance up, then when the time comes to make another decision, we will."

"Would you do that? I know you two had your heart set on buying some land."

"I love that old house. It's conveniently located downtown near the restaurants and bars, so that's good."

"Thank you, Mary. That's one problem solved. Jack is going to start on making the cottage ready for wheelchair accessibility, and putting in some handrails here and there, like in the shower. We'll need help with moving them. I know you are in serious wedding mode, but if we can get them here before the wedding, that would be terrific."

"No worries, just tell me when."

"Put the couch over there, by the window," Grandmother Lilly ordered. Jack and Danny put down the couch and began to walk away. "No, a little more this way," Grandmother said, motioning with her hand.

"A little higher," Patty said.

Annie obliged and slid the picture up the wall a little more. "Here?"

Patty took a couple of steps backward. "Just a smidgeon more."

After a full day of hanging pictures and rearranging furniture, Annie's eyes twinkled in amused interest as she looked around the room. The cottage, now warm and inviting, had a little bit of both Grandmother and Auntie in every room, and it made her happy deep inside.

"I think you'll both be very happy here. Jack has added some safety features for you. And, did you notice the custom rockers out front on the porch?"

Grandmother Lilly wrapped her thin arms around Jack's waist and hugged him close. "Thank you, dear. It's so lovely to have a nice strong man around the house."

"I know it's been a long day for you, but I do want to go over a few house rules with you."

Grandmother snorted. "House rules? Who do you think we are, college girls?"

Annie smirked. "No, but I don't want you cooking in here. Microwave only and the coffee maker."

"But I like to boil my water for tea on the stovetop," Patty complained.

"I'm sorry, Auntie Patty, but not anymore. You must use the microwave, or come up to the house and I'll make you tea."

"So, we must have all our meals with you guys, too?" Grandmother placed her hands on her hips.

Annie shook her head. "It's that, or we can have Meals on Wheels delivered."

"Is there any room for compromise with this?" Grandmother locked her eyes onto Annie's. The stare-down made her feel like a kid getting scolded by an adult.

"Maybe," Annie stuttered. "Let me think about it, but until we do come up with an alternative, please plan on eating with us."

"But tonight, we're having pizza," Jack said, breaking up the somber moment.

OVER THE NEXT TWO WEEKS, GRANDMOTHER AND AUNTIE settled in quite nicely, and only once did Annie and her grandmother disagree on something. Annie contacted an agency and had a woman come out to meet them. Grandmother and Auntie didn't put up any fuss, and understood she'd be there to help Annie. They came up with a schedule everyone could live with, and even included some meal preparation, which made Grand-mother and Auntie happy.

Annie fell onto her bed, both physically and mentally exhausted. The next hurdle would be Mary's wedding. She went over a few things in her mind before drifting off to sleep.

Jack didn't have the heart to wake her to change out of her clothes, so he just covered her with an afghan and quietly crawled in beside her. He leaned over and kissed her on the forehead.

With half-closed eyes, she smiled. "Love you," she whispered.

CHAPTER SEVENTEEN

A nnie ran to the window and looked outside. She lifted her hand and gave Mary a signal that she'd be right out. She rushed over to the small upholstered chair sitting in the corner of their bedroom and grabbed her purse.

"I'm off to help decorate the church," Annie said, leaning in and kissing Ashton then Jack.

"Have fun," he called out as he watched her dash out the door.

Annie pulled open the car door and sank into the rented van's heavily worn leather seat. Breathing hard, she placed her seat belt around her lap and chest. "Okay, let's go," she said, looking over at Mary.

Mary didn't put the car in gear. She turned slightly,

and with her back against the door she began to tap her fingers on the steering wheel.

"What? Why aren't we going?" Annie knitted her brows together.

"Ribbon? Bows?" Mary said, twisting her mouth to the left.

"Oh, geeze. I'll be right back." Annie pushed open the car door and headed toward the porch. Jack met her on the steps, holding a box filled with ribbon and bows. "Forget something?" He held it out to her.

"I'd forget my head ..." She took the box before finishing, holding it against her hip with one hand.

Jack leaned in and kissed her forehead. "Take a deep breath. Everything will be all right."

"See you in a few hours." Holding up her phone with her other hand, she added, "I remembered my phone, at least."

Jack tipped his head.

Annie tossed the box onto the back seat and then leapt back in where she'd been sitting earlier. "Okay, now I'm ready."

The girls chatted about Rebecca's new baby, about Grandmother and Auntie moving into the cottage, and about Danny and her upcoming move into the grand house downtown, which had been in their family for years and years.

"Dad was raised in that house," Mary said as she took the highway leading them to the church.

"Yes, we've made a lot of good memories in that house. I'm glad you guys are moving in."

Mary pulled into the long tree lined road. It was only the second time Annie had been there. She really took in the beautiful trees draped in moss, as well as the rest of the landscaping. She could imagine what the church would look like bustled with guests.

The two women headed to the back of the U-Haul van. Peering into the back, Mary said, "I'm so glad we found this lightweight aluminum arch. I love how you decorated it with floral swags in colors matching the other flowers."

"And using these painted masonry blocks to secure it was a great idea of Jack's," Annie said, lugging them to the porch.

The girls got busy putting the decorations in place and then stepped back to admire their work. Annie wrapped her arm around Mary. "It's beautiful, Sis," she said, pulling her in close.

"I don't know which part I like the best," Mary said, her eyes darting to the urns with the pussy willows to the candles that lined the window sills to the mono-grammed fabric aisle runner.

"One of my favorites is the wreath we made. The colors are so gorgeous," Annie said.

"Okay, I think our work is done here. Ready for the last stop?" Mary led the way out.

~

"THIS BACK ROOM IS PERFECT FOR US," ANNIE SAID, looking over the large banquet-size room.

"I set the tables up like this, but if you'd rather have it some other way, please feel free to move them," Rebecca said.

"No, I think this works."

"We just have a few things to bring in. Table decorations and some flowers and greenery for the bridal table, and then we'll be out of your hair," Mary said, heading outside.

Annie and Mary got to work. Soon every guest table was graced with a beautiful centerpiece with succulents. Floral swags draped the bridal party table and a candle centerpiece sat center of the table. A small round table at the entrance holding a framed picture of the happy couple along with a guest book and pen served as a guest sign in area. The cake table was also round, and had stacks of plates and silverware ready for the slicing of the layered delight. Although Danny and Mary had said no gifts, they set up a small table for those who would not follow instructions.

"I like the idea of the money tree," Mary said.

"Jack worked hard on that. It's so cute with all of its intricate branches," Annie said, helping her set it up. "It's really called the giving tree." Annie placed a small woven basket filled with clothespins near the tree.

The two women stepped back and admired their work. "Now, let's get home and get ready." Mary pulled her phone out of her pocket. "We have exactly three hours to get ready and get to that church!"

Annie and Mary jogged out of the restaurant, waving to Rebecca as they exited. "See you at the wedding," Mary called out.

Rebecca waved and smiled.

CHAPTER EIGHTEEN

J ack stood in front of the full-length mirror with his tongue slightly askew as he worked on his tie. "I wonder how they're doing in that small space?"

"What you really mean," Annie said, opening the closet door, "has Mary become one hot mess because of Grandmother and Auntie?" She pulled the dress she'd be wearing off its hanger and slipped it over her head.

"Got it," Jack said, turning around and showing off his neatly tied tie.

Annie tilted her head. "Good job," she said as she crossed to her jewelry box and retrieved the sapphire necklace and earring set Jack had given to her for her birthday. As she pulled the pieces out of the jewelry armoire that Jack had made her in his woodshop, she saw the pearls. Her hand flew to her mouth and she gasped. "I have to get these pearls to Mary."

"Your mother's?"

"Yes, something borrowed and something blue," she said.

"What will be the blue?"

"The garter," Annie said, smiling.

"Ah, the blue garter standby. Why does everyone use that for the blue item?"

"I guess because it's the easiest. I could let her wear the sapphire set. They're blue."

"Actually, they'd be borrowed and blue," Jack said. "You look lovely, by the way." He pulled her in and kissed her on the lips.

"Thank you. I still need to do my hair and makeup, but I better check on them," she said, eyeing her phone sitting on the bed.

Jack let her go from his grasp and watched as she picked up her phone. He sat on the bed and pulled on his socks and then put on his shoes, while she talked. He'd nod his head to the left and then to the right, smiling occasionally, and even letting out a small laugh. The conversation seemed to be going well.

"Thank goodness, all is well over at the granny unit." Annie dropped her phone on the bed beside them.

"Granny unit?"

"That's what Mary is calling it. Of course, if Grandmother hears mention of that, well, I don't want to be around if she does." Annie stood and slipped on the black strappy sandals placed near the bed.

"Twirl around for me," Jack said, leaning back on his arms and looking at her with half-closed lids. His sexy voice made the hair on the back of her neck stand.

She slowly turned around, making a complete circle and then stood with her hands clasped in front. "Well?"

"Beautiful." He extended his arms out for her to come to him.

"Jack, we have a wedding to get to. There's no time for this. And I have to wake Ashton up and get him ready. He has a very important part today."

"Just a little something to keep me going, please?" Jack pleaded with his eyes, making it impossible for her to refuse his request.

She took little steps toward him, lowering herself onto his lap. She wrapped her arms around his neck and gazed into his eyes. She pulled her hands up and ran her fingers through his thick hair and leaning down at the same time, gave him a kiss to remember.

"That's what I'm talking about. More from where that came from later, right?" He patted her on the butt.

Annie leaped from his lap. "That's just a little tease,"

she said as she exited the bedroom to get Ashton up and dressed.

~

"I'M HEADING OVER. WISH ME LUCK," ANNIE SAID WITH one hand on the doorknob.

"Good luck," Jack called out as he and Ashton sat on the sofa. "We gotta get going, though. It will take us forty minutes to get there. Tell them to hurry up," he said, looking at his watch.

~

SHE COULD HEAR THE BANTERING FROM THE PORCH. SHE drew in a deep breath and stepped inside. The small cottage looked like the inside of a dressing room. Lingerie was draped over the back of chairs, curling iron and blow dryers were placed on tables, makeup bags were strewn over the sofa cushions, and shoes ... shoes were everywhere.

"Why so many pairs of shoes?" Annie asked.

"Grandmother couldn't decide between the flats, the heels, or the moccasin-style shoes," Mary said, stepping into her wedding dress.

Annie crossed over to her and helped by zipping the

back. "Okay, but couldn't y'all put some stuff away? This is a serious tripping hazard."

"Tripping hazard?" Grandmother blurted. "This isn't a daycare, I resent that," she said, tsk-tsking in disapproval.

"I didn't mean anything derogatory by that, Grandmother. Anyone can trip over items. And we don't need any broken hips."

Annie turned back toward Mary. "Listen, I know we were going with the blue garter and Mom's pearls for something borrowed." Annie held up the string of pearls. "But, I was wondering if you'd like to wear my sapphire necklace and earrings instead, and they could be both your something blue and something borrowed. Jack and I would love for you to wear them."

"Oh, Annie, that would be awesome," Mary said, stepping toward her with open arms.

Annie hugged her, while holding the jewelry in her hands. She chuckled a bit and then stepped back. "Turn around and I'll put the necklace on."

"You look stunning, Mary," Auntie Patty said.

"All right, let me give everyone a quick check and then we have to be going," Annie said, working her eyes from Grandmother to Auntie and then finally back to Mary. She straightened the collar on Grandmother's blouse, clipped a couple of stray hairs that had come down from Patty's chignon, and then grabbing the box with Mary's veil, she scooted everyone out the door.

～

MARY PACED THE LITTLE ROOM THE SIZE OF AN OVERSIZE utility closet, which also served as her waiting room. Located in the front of the church, it meant they'd have to exit the room via a side door, and walk around to the entrance when the time came. Crystal and Ashton were given last-minute instructions. Everyone loved kids in weddings, so no matter how bad things went, it wouldn't ruin the day.

"Mary, calm down. Everything will be all right," Annie said in a low and soft tone.

"Is he here yet?"

Annie opened the door a crack and peered into the church. Her eyes landed on Grandmother, then Patty. Then her eyes traveled to another section where she found Rebecca, Michael, Vicky, and Scott. *No Danny.* "The guests are trickling in," Annie said, keeping alarm out of her voice.

"Danny? Do you see Danny? How about his parents?"

Annie's breath caught then she swallowed. She opened the door, once again, and peered out. More guests were arriving each minute, each second. Her eyes grew big when she saw Milly, Robert, Preston, and Susan walk in ... with Danny! "Yes, Danny is here. So are his parents and Jack's."

Mary began to tremble and a tear escaped her lid.

"Aw, Mary, don't cry. This is the day you've been waiting for. I'm so happy for you and Danny."

"I wish Mom and Dad were here. But, we've been through all this before. The only thing we're missing is Grandmother and Auntie back here."

Annie looked around the small space. "Fortunately there is no room. We don't need any drama today." Her hand covered her mouth as she tried to suppress a giggle.

The girls' ears perked up when the music began to play. "That's the be-ready-in-five-minutes music," Mary stammered.

Annie reached down and grabbed Ashton's and Crystal's hands and they exited the small room.

As the two women made their way, Annie briefly thought about how she played an important role in Mary's wedding. It wasn't every day that a big sister had the privilege of giving away her little sister. They stopped just before getting to the door.

Annie retrieved the little wagon decorated in white lace and hot glued flowers that Jack had set outside for them, and sat Ashton inside. She handed him the little wooden box holding the rings. She gave Crystal the bag of rose petals and gave her a quick rundown of her job. The little girl nodded that she understood.

"I love the wreath we made," Mary said, nodding toward their creation of miniature silk flowers in an array of colors from burnt orange to yellow with a splash of green, all tied up with a beautiful satiny bow.

"I do, too." Annie stepped toward the door and placed her ear against it. "It's playing. The wedding march is playing." She skipped over to Mary and quickly lowered her veil. "Ready?" Her eyes twinkled as she handed her the bouquet of burnt orange colored roses with baby's breath and feathery ferns, all tied up with a dark green satiny ribbon.

Mary nodded.

Annie pulled open the door and motioned for Crystal to pick up the wagon handle and enter the church. The creaking sounds of bodies turning on old wooden benches and shoes making scrapping sounds, along with *oohs* and *ahhs*, did nothing to curtail their nerves. However, the two women made their way down the aisle, nodding and smiling as they followed the rose petals to the front where both the minister and Danny waited. Both of them had beads of sweat forming on their brows.

"Danny is sweating," Mary said through gritted teeth.

"It's a little warm in here," Annie whispered back.

Annie passed Mary off to Danny, and then stood to the side.

Mary reached up and dabbed Danny's brow with the hankie Grandmother had given her. He winked at her and a few sweet sounds came from the pews. Everyone loved Mary's gesture.

Mary and Danny had written their own vows, so after each of them spoke from memory, the preacher finished by blessing the union and then announced them as husband and wife.

And ... when it came time to retrieve the rings ... Ashton hadn't flung them out of the wagon like a ball. He actually handed them very nicely, and very much like a big boy to Uncle Danny. Jack and Annie were so proud.

～

ANNIE KNEW MARY AND DANNY WERE HOLDING BACK something they'd been working on. No matter how much she'd tried to knock it out of Mary, she wouldn't budge. "It's a surprise," she'd repeat over and over. So when it came time to make the toast to the newlyweds and they'd disappeared from the reception, Annie got a bit worried. Then the music started and everyone looked up when the two came dancing through the door to a song they found special. They tapped their guests on the shoulders as they passed them to join in the dance, and soon, the entire room danced to the catchy tune. It couldn't have come off any better had each guest rehearsed it with them. The energy of the room, the spirit of the melody, and the nuance of the words sung, only intensified the moment and it would go down in the McPherson girls' history as one of the most entertaining receptions ever.

Annie tapped her water glass to get everyone's attention after the group dance. "I don't know how I'll top that, but I do want to say a few words to Mary and Danny."

The group clapped.

"Mary," she said, locking her gaze onto hers. "You know you are very special to me. You're more than a sister, you're my friend. I love you and I'm so happy for you."

Then she turned to Danny. "And, Danny, you better take good care of her, or you'll have to deal with the mean big sister side of me, and I don't think you want that." She snickered and then winked at him.

Danny tilted his chin up and down and raised his glass. He mouthed he'd do just that.

"Seriously, though, I love you both, and, Danny, welcome to the family!"

The guests erupted in cheers and clapped. Then the DJ turned up the tunes again, and everyone soon began dancing.

A slow song played and Jack grabbed Annie's hands and pulled her willingly to the dance floor. He leaned in deep and pulled her close. "I told you it would be all right."

Annie tilted her head back, and lowering her lids, she pulled in her bottom lip. A sigh escaped her lips. "You're always right, Jack. Didn't you know that?" With half-closed lids she moved in for his kiss.

"Wait." He stopped her. "Did you say I'm always right?"

Annie stopped swaying her hips when a *humph* sound escaped her lips. "Right or wrong, it's my job to make you think you're always right."

"Okay, I can live with that." He grabbed her hands and pulled her back in. "As long as you don't lie about anything else, we're good." He stood his ground, searching her face for approval.

"I'd never lie to you, Jack. I just don't ever want to fight with you."

"Fight? No, but disagree, always." Jack dropped a kiss on her mouth.

"Why disagree?" Annie knitted her brows.

"Because, me man, you woman. That's the way it is." He let out a low belly laugh.

"Jack Powell," Annie said, shaking her head at him. Then she pulled him in and they swayed to the music as she rested her head on his shoulder, drinking in his scent that drove her absolutely wild.

CHAPTER NINETEEN

A nnie moved on to the next big thing in her life, after all the fanfare of Mary and Danny's wedding blew over—the holidays. And they were coming at her full speed ahead. First came Jack's birthday. They always celebrated it, usually with some sort of party at their house. He loved to make big bonfires and have everyone sit around and tell ghost stories, and since his birthday was on Halloween, it felt like a normal thing to do.

She hadn't really discussed it with him yet, but she thought she'd invite Danny and Mary, Vicky and Scott, and now that they'd reconnected, maybe she would throw out an invite to the pinky sisters as they were now affectionately known. And of course, Grandmother and Auntie; she would work them in to the party, and they could just stay until they got tired. That was the advantage to having them live on property.

She'd been feeling a bit tired, but who wouldn't with all that she had going on. She'd just submitted a huge order for supplies via the internet for the bakery. *Boy, Mary will be happy about me doing more online.* Annie hit the submit key and leaned back. Her eyes went to the front door when she heard the commotion.

"We just had the best time," Jack said, bringing in the cool autumn air as he shut the door. Ashton giggled and then ran to his mom, hugging her legs.

"Mommy," Ashton cried, burying his face in her lap.

"Did you have a good time with Daddy?" She patted his back.

Ashton pulled up his head and grinned.

"Hey, I was just thinking about your birthday. What do you think about a simple cookout with a few friends, nothing too big?" Annie raised her brows and waited for Jack's reply.

"We don't have to do anything this year. We've had a few already this year and we've attended a few. Let's just go out to dinner, you and me." He sat down next to her.

Annie tilted her head and studied his face. "Seriously? No party? But it's Halloween."

"I know, but let's do something different. We can ask Mary and Danny to babysit. Let's take the boat and go to the restaurant we went to when we were dating. It's been ages since we've been there, and we really haven't broken in the new *Lady Powell* enough."

Annie's mind drifted to the old *Lady Powell* and how Jack loved his boat so much. They'd had a lot of good times riding the waterways. When the hurricane ripped a hole the size of a watermelon in her, Jack had to turn her into scrap metal, and now a beautiful new boat docked in her place. *Lady Powell*, the second.

"The weather is supposed to change from cold to balmy. I think a boat ride on the moonlit water would be delightful. I'll call Mary right now."

ANNIE WORE A PAIR OF HER DARKEST JEANS AND A sleeveless blouse under a thick cable stitched sweater. She wrapped a chiffon scarf around her hair and neck, and boarded the boat. Jack had on his newest pair of jeans and a baby blue polo shirt and a lightweight windbreaker. The forecast had been correct, and it would be a very enjoyable evening for a boat ride.

Jack motored into the berth and cut the engine, while Annie held the steering wheel. He hopped out onto the dock and tied *Lady Powell* up. Annie turned off the idling motor and then gathered her things. Jacked extended his hand to help her out. She squeezed it slightly as she pulled herself up onto the dock. She untied the scarf from her head and moved it to her neck, tying it off in a nice fancy knot. She laced her arm in his and they walked the several feet down the dock and up the ramp that led them to the restaurant.

Once inside, the hostess seated them at the window. While they looked over the menu, they asked for a bottle of wine to be brought to them. Annie leaned over the menu and whispered, "It's been ages since we've been on a date. I feel naughty almost."

Jack closed the menu. "Keep the thought close by." He started to say something else, but the server brought their bottle of wine. She pulled the foil wrapper off with a fancy wine tool, then popped the cork. She poured a small amount into a glass and handed it to Jack. Jack drew in a whiff through his nostrils, then twirled the glass and drew in a second smell, really drawing in the sweet bouquet, and then he tasted it. "This is very good," he said, holding his glass out for more.

The server filled both of their glasses and then took their order.

After they ate dinner, they took their half-finished bottle of wine and headed down to the boat. But not before Jack drew Annie into his arms and kissed her so passionately she folded like a blanket in his arms. She pulled her hands up his back and raked her nails lightly, but enough to bring him to moan softly in her ear. She then pushed her hands up toward his neck and then into his hair as she deepened the kiss. Gasping they pulled apart.

"Wow, that was some kiss," Jack said, brushing his hand through his hair.

"It must be the wine," Annie said, breathing heavily.

"It's the wine, it's the date, it's us," he said, pulling her in for one last kiss.

JACK AND ANNIE ENTERED THE HOUSE, HOLDING HANDS TO find Danny and Mary snuggled on the couch, watching the home decorating channel.

"How was dinner?" Mary said, moving out of Danny's embrace.

"It was sooo good," Annie purred.

"How was the boat ride?" Danny asked.

"It was sooo good," Jack said, looking over at Annie and smiling.

"How was Ashton?" Annie said, trying to break away from Jack's spellbinding gaze.

"He was sooo good," Mary said, emphasizing the word like they had.

Annie and Jack belted out a laugh. "We're sorry. It's just been such a long time since we've been alone, out on a date. We really should try to do it more often. It really helps with the marriage connection," Jack said, blushing.

Danny and Mary rose from the couch. "Anytime," Danny said.

"Oh, by the way, Grandmother called five times tonight." Mary said, reaching for her sweater hanging on the back of a chair.

"Is everything all right? I stopped in there before we left for dinner," Annie said with a puzzled look on her face.

"Yes, everything is okay. They were feeling a bit lonely, so I went over there and curled their hair, and gave them each a manicure."

"Ashton and I hung out here with Isla and Buffy," Danny said, wrapping his arm around Mary.

Mary cuddled against his chest. "Yeah, he's trying to see how this daddy thing works. You know, in case we want to give it a try."

Annie's eyes widened. "Well, I'd love to be an auntie, so anytime."

"Just promise me you won't be like our Auntie," Mary said, crossing toward the front door.

"Well, Auntie isn't so bad, it's Grandmother," Annie said.

"I love your grandmother," Danny said, sticking out his chest. "She's a hoot."

"She is that," Mary said, laughing.

The four walked out onto the front porch. Jack wrapped his arm around Annie and the two watched as Mary and Danny made their way toward their car. "You kids, drive safe. The roads are dark out here in the country," Jack called.

Annie waved. "Call me tomorrow, Mary."

They watched them drive away and then then Jack turned to Annie. "I didn't think they'd ever leave."

Annie laughed. "I know."

Jack stepped closer. The moonlight danced off the water and seemed to bounce off the grove of trees on the property. He could see a hint of it in her eyes. He drew her in for a long kiss and just as before, she folded in his arms like a big warm blanket.

CHAPTER TWENTY

After Jack's birthday, came Thanksgiving. Annie had pledged she'd host all the parties, taking some of the burden off of Milly.

Jack helped Annie insert the two large leaves into the wood table he'd built. She tossed one end of the red tablecloth to him and they stretched it out, covering the table. She immediately went to work placing the centerpiece she and Mary had made, a cornucopia filled with small lifelike gourds and silk flowers. When the two had decorated the church and made the swags and other embellishments, it got them onto the path of making more crafts. Now, even Sweet Magnolia had a big beautiful wreath hanging on its front door, as well as one at the granny cottage.

Jack opened the china cabinet door and began to

retrieve the plates. Soon, each chair boasted a beautiful setting of white china rimmed in gold and complementary silverware, neatly arranged on top of matching red linen napkins. Annie stepped back and admired the table.

"Okay, so I have everything either in the oven or ready to go. The turkey is ready for the fryer after the men get here," she said with her hands on her hips and her bottom lip pulled in.

"What else is there?" Jack asked with a bewildered look on his face.

"The turkey platter, can you get that down for me?"

Jack went to where they kept the step stool and headed for the cabinet over the refrigerator.

Robert, Preston, Jack, Richard, Danny, and Scott stood outside, huddled around the large turkey fryer. The women and children stayed inside. Ashton and his cousin Crystal played nicely on the living room floor. Even though she was older, she didn't seem to be bothered by having to entertain him. Once Vicky and Scott came over with Jasmine, Ashton had two little girl playmates. He didn't seem to mind either.

The women sat around the dining room table, chatting and glad to be inside sheltered from the cold. The fire glowed in the living room, and both Isla and Buffy were curled in their beds, soaking in the warmth from the flickering flames,

The back door flew open and Jack peered around the corner. "Ten more minutes," he called out.

Annie rose up from her chair and crossed over to the kitchen.

"Need help, Sis?"

"Can you do me a favor and go get Grandmother and Auntie?"

"It will take them five minutes just to get to the front door," Mary said.

Annie turned her back on Mary and opened the oven door. The wonderful smells of cinnamon and sugar wafted through the room. She pulled out the large dish with the sweet potato casserole and set it on the trivet on the counter.

"Smells so good in there," Milly called out. "Sure you don't need any help?" She stood just on the outskirts of the kitchen, waiting for an invitation to enter.

"Well, if you could get the cranberry sauce out of the fridge and the Watergate salad, that would be great."

Milly began to fulfill the tasks Annie had asked her to do. When she finished, she stood like a soldier awaiting her next set of orders.

Annie handed her a set of potholders. "The green bean casserole and sweet potato casserole can go on the table."

Soon the men entered the house with the steaming bird. All eyes were on the turkey as it made its way into the kitchen, the skin a crispy brown.

Jack sliced up the turkey after it had rested for a few minutes, despite everyone chomping at the bit. The rest of the side dishes formed a line down the center of the huge dining room table.

"Dinner is served," Jack called out, carrying the heavy turkey platter to the table.

Annie reached for her tablemates hands, and thus began the chain of handholding. "Dear Father, thank you for the food we're about to enjoy. Thank you so much for letting me be the host this year, and continue to bless us with your grace. Amen."

The mumblings of amens went around the table, and then all you could hear were the clanging of utensils on china and the sound of joyful bantering. The Powells and McPhersons were in the house!

～

EVERYONE SAT AROUND HOLDING THEIR SIDES AND moaning. As usual, they'd overeaten.

"Coffee and dessert, anyone?" Annie winced as she waited for the rebuttals.

More groans came, mostly from the women.

"I'll take a slice of pumpkin, with just a small dollop of whipped cream," Robert called out.

"I'll second that," Jack said.

Annie slowly made her way into the kitchen to slice the pie. After they'd passed out the desserts to all the men and Grandmother and Patty, Annie approached the subject of the next upcoming holiday, Christmas.

Standing at the backside of the sofa and giving Jack a shoulder massage, Annie watched on. "I don't know how you have room for that pie, Grandmother."

"I just say the word dessert and my brain promptly makes room for it."

The entire room broke out into laughter.

"I had a few ideas for Christmas. Does anyone want to hear them?" Annie smiled at the group in the living room, and then turned her eyes to the rest who had stayed seated at the dining room table. Susan, Danny's mother, made a noise, and then when all eyes were on her, she shrugged her shoulders as if she didn't mean anything by it. She clearly did.

"I do," Mary quipped, quirking her brows at her mother-in-law.

"I thought it would be nice to drive through the light

display on James Island. We haven't done that in years. Now that Ashton is bigger, he'd really enjoy that. They have a small skating area, a gift store, and they serve hot chocolate. We could go out and have a nice dinner at California Dreaming and then head over to the light show. What do you say?" Annie nodded to the groups.

"You young people go do that. It might be too much for Patty and me," Lilly said as she forked her last bite of the pumpkin delight.

"Speak for yourself, Lilly. I want to go," Patty said with a girlish smile on her face.

Grandmother cut her a wild look, then licked her fork one last time.

"I also thought about a tree cutting day, but I know every family may have their own tradition regarding that. Anyone is welcome to go with us when we go, though."

"Artificial," Lilly blurted.

"Artificial? You mean you want an artificial tree for the granny ... I mean the cottage?" Mary yelled from the other room.

"Lilly, there's nothing better than the scent of a fresh tree. I want a fresh tree. It might be our last year to ever have one," Patty said, now cutting her a wild look.

"Now, now, you two, this is not going to be your last year, so let's stop with that sort of talk. Secondly, we could always cut down a small tree, Grandmother. Would that be okay?" Annie raised her brow, waiting for Grandmother to reply.

"Oh, all right, I guess, I'm always outvoted it seems."

"I'm happy to host Christmas Eve dinner here. We could do something light, like maybe hearty appetizers and snacks. We can play games and watch old movies."

"*It's a Wonderful Life*," Robert said.

"Oh, I know, let's go downtown and take a carriage ride and visit the marketplace during the holidays. We can make it an early day, and have lunch downtown. It's so pretty downtown during the holidays," Mary said, changing the subject.

"Okay, I like that idea. I don't know how many carriages we can reserve, though. How many are interested in doing that?" Annie counted hands.

Jack, Danny, Mary, Richard, Diane, Vicky, and Scott were the only ones who raised their hands.

"Okay, so I'll check on that, then," Annie said, making a mental note of everything she'd willingly said she'd do. Turning her attention to the older group, Annie made eye contact with Robert's and Milly's parents first. "Is there anything special you'd like to do for the holidays?"

"Just be with family," Bert Powell said in his raspy voice.

"I agree. We just love being around you all. Makes us feel fifty-two instead of eighty-two," Cora Wiggins, Milly's mother said.

Eighty-Two, wow, that means Grandmother and Auntie are nearing eighty. "And we love having you," Annie said, her eyes misting.

Milly's dad, Russell shifted his weight in the over-stuffed chair. "I think if we just get together a few times during the season, all of us old folks would be good with it," his eyes wandered left to right and then rested back on Annie's.

Annie tipped her head. "Then, that's what we'll do."

"I know," Patty said, waving her hand around.

Annie nodded at her.

"I'd like to host a little something at the granny cottage."

Annie's eyes darted to Mary and then back to Patty. "Granny Cottage? How?"

"You don't think we don't know that's what you girls are calling, it did you?" She breathed deeply before continuing. "Just Polly, Bert, Russell, and Cora. We can have a nice lunch together. Maybe play some cards?"

Annie chuckled. She had to hand it to Grandmother and Auntie. They would not stop living life until their last breath. "Okay, let's set that up."

～

MARY AND DANNY ESCORTED GRANDMOTHER AND AUNTIE back to the cottage. Jack and Annie waved goodbye to Milly and Robert who had Russell, Cora, Polly, and Bert with them. Vicky, Scott, and Jasmine walked Robert, Diane, and Crystal to their car, and then continued the short walking distance to their home. Susan and Preston had been the first ones to leave and hardly anyone had noticed. Annie and Jack stood on the porch, with Jack holding a very sleepy Ashton over his shoulder, and watched as all the car lights disappeared into the darkness. Annie reached out and lightly rubbed Jack's arm. "What a great Thanksgiving, huh?"

"I'd say it will go down in history as one of the best. It was great to have everyone here."

"I'm exhausted," Annie stepped inside the house and motioned for Jack to come in. "Please put him to bed. I'll finish cleaning up the kitchen and meet you in the bedroom." She rose up on her tiptoes and kissed Ashton on the top of the head.

Annie slowly made her way into the kitchen with low slung shoulders to find the mile high stack of dishes waiting for her. She sighed loudly, then began to scrape, rinse, and stack the dishes in the dishwasher. She'd only done a few when she heard Jack come in.

He grabbed the sponge out of her hand and smiled. "Go get ready for bed, I'll finish up."

Annie furrowed her brows. "Huh? No, let's knock it out together." She swiped the sponge back out of his hands.

Jack laughed. "Okay, let's tackle this together like we do everything."

Soon the dishes were all done, and both of them were snoring softly, dreaming of the great family dinner.

∼

It took a little bit of motivation on Annie's part, but she got Grandmother and Patty to agree with the tree cutting trip. She helped them layer up with warm clothing, and then Jack met them outside the cottage with the truck.

They found a small Charlie Brown type tree for them and a seven foot blue spruce for themselves. The place they went to served hot chocolate, so while the staff carried the trees to the bed of the truck and securely tied them in, the five of them sipped on hot chocolate and scanned the aisles of the small gift store where Auntie Patty purchased a small ornament for their new tree.

"How about we get pizza for dinner?" Jack suggested as he pulled out of the tree farm.

After pizza, Annie announced she needed to give Ashton a bath. Jack took the cue and offered to get both Grandmother and Auntie, as well as their small tree home. He'd been gone a while. In fact, Ashton had finished his bath, was in his pajamas, and was looking at a book on the sofa when Jack finally returned.

"What took you so long?" Annie placed her hands on her hips and smiled. She figured they'd asked him to do something.

"Well, let's see. The lightbulb was burned out in the bathroom, the front door squeaked when it opened and closed, and then I had to bring the tree in and set it up."

A low belly laugh, turning into something a bit more hysterical, came out of Annie's mouth. "Those two, they just love you so much, Jack."

"Tomorrow, I promised to help decorate the tree," Jack said, hanging his head low.

Annie grabbed her sides from laughing so hard. "They have you wrapped around their little fingers."

Just as he'd promised, Jack helped decorate the little tree. When he came back to the main house, Annie quickly became suspicious of his overly flirtatious behavior. She sniffed him. "Jack Powell! It's not even five o'clock and you smell like booze."

"It's five o'clock somewhere," he said, pulling her in and kissing her mouth passionately.

She tried to resist him by placing her hands on his chest, but it was no use. She drooped right into his arms like week old daisies. After they kissed, she stepped back and with her hands on her hips she asked, "What kind of booze did they have over there? I don't recall buying them anything."

"Now, you know your grandmother and auntie like their wine and scotch. Nothing's changed. And I do believe your sister may have had a hand in the eggnog."

"Eggnog?"

Jack nodded. "Loaded with brandy." His eyes twinkled, and then he stepped forward and pulled her right back in for another kiss.

~

ANNIE BEGAN CHECKING THINGS OFF ON HER CALENDAR. The next big thing on the list was the card party at the cottage with all the grandparents.

"I want those little pinwheel sandwiches," Lilly said, seated at the dining room table with Patty and Annie.

Annie launched the color note app on her phone, another cool feature she'd discovered, and began to make a grocery list. "Chicken pâté for the spread?" She looked up to see Patty nodding.

"Fresh veggies are too hard for us to eat with all of our false teeth," Lilly said.

"False teeth? Speak for yourself. I have all of my teeth," Patty said, squaring her shoulders and sitting up straighter.

Lilly playfully slapped air toward her and then grunted. "How about some boiled shrimp and cocktail sauce? Everyone should be able to gum them." She let out a snarky laugh.

"Grandmother," Annie scolded. "Be nice. Okay, so pinwheel sandwiches, shrimp with cocktail sauce, and how about some Christmas cookies or brownies as a sweet treat?"

"How about some cupcakes, instead?" Patty raised her brows almost to her hairline.

"Cupcakes! Oh, my. I haven't even thought about Sweet Indulgence for one second. I've been so preoccupied with hosting parties that I've forgotten about my beloved bakery and my supportive and loyal staff." Annie hung her head low and wept.

"Now, now, child, you didn't forget about them. You've just been a bit preoccupied, as you say, but it's not too late. I tell you what, let's all make a trip into town and pick out the cupcakes. We can take some Christmas cheer into the bakery and make the day of your employees. Let them know you've not forgotten about them." Lilly reached out and cupped Annie's hand.

"I'd like that, thank you," she whispered.

⁓

THE THREE OF THEM STOPPED BY A COUPLE OF STORES AND had some items gift wrapped. Annie purchased some gift cards from the local bookstore and coffee shop, as well as the movie theater, and then placed them in Christmas cards addressed to each employee. When the three of them entered the bakery, Annie's eyes widened and Grandmother and Patty gasped. The place was decorated with red shiny bobbles, silver strands of beads, and greenery. Words like "Noel" and "Peace on Earth" were written in spray snow on the windows, and a small tree, complete with lights and ornaments, sat in the corner. Even wrapped up boxes placed around the tree skirt gave a nice finishing touch to the warmly decorated space.

"Hey, Ms. Powell," Peter called out as he stepped around the counter.

"Peter, you decorated the shop."

"I hope you don't mind? I found the items in the back storage room. We had a blast decorating. I know you've been busy." He nodded to Grandmother and Auntie.

"Well, I have been a bit preoccupied, but I wanted to stop by and bring some cheer. Actually, it was their idea." She turned and smiled at Lilly and Patty.

Peter reached out and took the two large baskets and placed them on the counter. "This is so thoughtful of you. I'll make sure each of them get their gift."

"We also would like to purchase some cupcakes. We're having a little party at our place and nothing says sweet like a cupcake," Patty said, beaming ear to ear.

"Step on up to the display case and let me know what you'd like. I know the owner and I think I can get you a good deal." He winked at Annie.

Grandmother and Patty picked out enough cupcakes to feed an army, and Annie let them. They were having so much fun.

"Listen, we're getting together for dinner at Black Eyed Pea on the twenty-first. I know it's a few days before Christmas, but we're trying to fit in so many things. Rebecca and Michael will be there. I know she'd love to see you. I'll reach out to Morgan, as well. In fact, invite all the employees. It's on me and Jack." Annie's chest swelled with happiness.

Annie ushered Grandmother and Auntie out of the bakery and into the parked car right out front. Once seated and belted, she let out a sigh of relief. "That went really well." She leaned her head back and rested it on the headrest which extended above her seat.

"It really did. And the last-minute dinner invitation was a great idea," Patty said from the back seat.

"It didn't come off sounding like it was last-minute, did it?"

"Not really, besides, you know young people. They don't plan anything," Lilly said.

"Okay. Hold on to those cupcakes, Patty. We're off," Annie said as she checked the side mirrors before pulling away from the curb.

"EVERYONE ACCOUNTED FOR?" ANNIE ASKED JACK WHEN he returned from the cottage.

"Yup. Mom said for us to call them about forty-five minutes before it ends so they can pick them all up."

Annie looked at her watch. "Okay. How'd Grandmother and Auntie seem?"

"Fine. I think a little nervous, but they are getting a kick out of entertaining. You know, you can take the Charlestonian out of Charleston, but you can't take their love of entertaining away. It follows them wherever they go, even to the granny cottage." Jack's somber face soon turned into a wide smile and both he and Annie broke out into laughter.

"I plan to go over in a bit and check on them," Annie said.

~

ANNIE QUIETLY OPENED THE DOOR AND SAID HELLO. THE group sat around the table playing cards and bantering back and forth. Christmas carols played in the background. With the tree lit up, and the few decorations placed around the cottage, it appeared rather festive, pleasing Annie immensely.

"Annie, come in. Want to play a hand of gin rummy with us?" Patty shuffled the deck and motioned for Annie to take a seat.

"Sure, just one quick round."

"Would you like some eggnog?" Lilly asked, sliding out her chair.

No wonder all the smiles. Everyone was a bit tipsy on Grandmother's nog. "Do you have any without brandy?"

~

"I WAS ABOUT TO SEND OUT THE DOGS. YOU'VE BEEN GONE a while," Jack said with a look of concern on his face.

"They talked me into playing cards. It was fun. And you're right, Grandmother is sharing her brandy laced nog with everyone. I better warn Milly." She reached for her cell phone.

"I'll walk over there when I see them come up the drive. They might need some help piling those light-headed folks into the car," Jack said with pursed lips.

Annie pulled in her bottom lip and nodded back.

AT THE LAST MINUTE, LITTLE JASMINE CAME DOWN WITH A cold, so Vicky and Scott opted out of the carriage ride, leaving just Danny, Mary, Jack, Annie, Richard, and Diane. They dropped off Ashton over at Milly and Robert's, and picked up Richard and Diane. They left Crystal with Milly, as well. The six of them headed downtown where a carriage awaited them.

The clopping noise of hooves on cobblestone lulled the group into a peaceful silence, and as the horse-drawn carriage made its way up and down the streets, they took in the simply decorated Charleston homes, many with just wreaths and greenery. Wide red ribbon and big bows draped lampposts, and the occasional white delicate twinkling lights strung in windows gave off a luminous glow. While snuggled under red plaid blankets and sipping on cups of coffee, the group of friends toured Charleston as if it were their first time.

"That was so much fun," Diane said. "I have suggested this tour a thousand times, maybe even more, and yet this is my first time doing it."

"I know, it's right here in our neighborhood and we forget to play tourist ourselves," Mary said in agreement.

"Where to next, tour guide?" Jack said, nodding toward Annie.

"The marketplace!"

The most famous for sweetgrass basketry, the marketplace showcased some of the most beautiful handicrafts of African origin. Annie had her eye on a very elegant one and immediately wanted to buy it for Mary. "Jack," Annie whispered.

Jack playfully nudged her and leaned in.

"I want to get this basket for Mary. Keep her away, while I make the purchase."

Jack nodded. He searched the marketplace, and when he caught a glimpse of her and Danny, he made a beeline toward them.

Annie picked up the small brown basket with a handle made out of the locally harvested marsh grass, which grew wild in the low country, and admired it. *This was a true handicraft.* She asked the clerk to box it up. As she made her way to the next booth, a pair of dangling earrings made of abalone shell caught her eye. She immediately thought of Auntie Patty. No matter how old they were, they still liked to dress in style. When Annie came across the booth displaying hats, she knew the perfect gift for Grandmother. With bags looped over each arm, Annie caught up with the rest of the group. "I'm famished. Ready to go eat?"

"What's in the bags?" a nosey Mary asked, nudging one of the bags with her hands.

Annie lifted the bag away from her reach. "Hands off," she joked.

The group walked the two blocks to the restaurant, and over shrimp and grits and other Charleston favorites, the friends enjoyed the good food and conversation.

"What a great holiday treat," Jack said, lifting his glass for a toast.

∼

WHILE JACK AND ANNIE LAY IN BED, LISTENING TO THE dogs snore softly from their beds, they reminisced about the carriage ride and shopping trip.

Jack pulled his arm out from under the bedding and

guided it under her head, pulling her closer. "So, let's see. We've done the tree cutting, the grandparents booze party, and the downtown carriage ride." He moved his hand up to her head and ran his hand through her hair.

She snuggled deeper into him. "We have the lights at James Island and dinner at California Dreaming on Wednesday, and then the last thing before Christmas Eve is when we're meeting everyone at Black Eyed Pea on the twenty-first."

Soft snores came from Jack's side of the bed.

"Jack? Jack did you hear me?" Annie rolled slightly up on one elbow and gazed at Jack. She dropped back down and closed her eyes. It had been a long day.

~

"I'm so happy Jasmine is feeling better. I know she'll love the Christmas lights," Annie said on the phone with Vicky.

"We're looking forward to dinner, too. See you in a bit. Are you sure you don't mind driving?" Vicky asked.

"Not at all, we borrowed one of the limos so we can see the lights in style."

There were lights shaped like boats, lights shaped like bridges, and lights designed after well-known characters. After they toured the massive display, they parked the car at the gift store area, where Ashton and Jasmine tried their skill at ice-skating. Ashton did pretty well for a youngin. Then they sipped some hot chocolate and roasted some marshmallows. When Ashton begged Jack to put his third marshmallow on the metal roasting tool, Annie mentioned it might be time to go eat dinner.

Just as she'd suspected, neither Ashton nor Jasmine were really hungry with bellies full of marshmallows and hot chocolate. At Christmas time, all rules went out the window it seemed. The parents convinced them to at least share some chicken strips.

Annie enjoyed her grilled fish and Jack *oohed* and *ahhed* over his baby back ribs. Vicky had their famous California Dreaming salad, known to be gigantic, and Scott had a rib eye steak cooked to perfection, pink in the center, just the way he liked it. After dinner, they drove back to Kiawah where Jack decided it would be a great night for a bonfire.

"Ashton is all tucked in and Isla and Buffy are on guard duty," she said, snuggling next to him as he poked the fire.

"It's a beautiful night. It's so clear, you can see all the stars," he said, looking up into the dark and immense sky.

"I had a lovely evening. I'm so happy Vicky and Scott

were able to join us tonight. I think Jasmine had a blast, too," Annie said, resting her arm on his leg.

He cupped her hand with his and squeezed it. "We're truly blessed, that's for sure."

Annie's eyes darted to a movement she saw near some trees. "*Shh*, look, a deer." She nodded toward the grove of trees to the right of them. They both watched as two deer slowly inched their way deeper into the property, then losing sight of them completely.

Jack moved his hand and ran it up her back, resting it right at the nape of her neck. She shivered. "Are you cold?" He pulled her closer.

"Not really, when you touch me, something happens. No matter where we are at, you do something to me that I can't explain." She studied every inch of his face.

"I feel it, too. I guess we have a strong connection." He lowered his eyes to her mouth, causing the heat to rise to her face.

She inched a bit closer. "Kiss me," she whispered.

He cupped her face and drew her in closer, and before he found her mouth to kiss her, he sighed. "You are more beautiful each day. I don't know how that's possible, but it is." He moved closer and their lips met. She relaxed her shoulders, not realizing how stiff she'd become.

He deepened the kiss more, and just when she opened her mouth to let him know she wanted more, a squeaky door opened and a voice called out, "Get a room." Then the door shut loudly.

Both Jack and Annie burst out laughing. "I thought you said you fixed that door?"

CHAPTER TWENTY-ONE

A nnie grew more excited about the dinner at Black Eyed Pea, and the final to-do item on her holiday list, than any other event thus far. It would be the day the pinky sisters returned for their agreed upon visit, and her loyal and loving staff of Sweet Indulgence, and of course, her husband Jack, would all attend.

Rebecca and her restaurant staff went all-out to provide a very tasty holiday meal, complete with turnip greens, homemade biscuits, and pork chops smothered in mushrooms and onions. For dessert, Rebecca's grandmother carried out the prettiest pineapple upside down cake ever.

Annie clinked her water glass with her spoon. Once all eyes were on her, she stood. "Thank you so much for coming tonight. Thank you to Rebecca for letting us crash your restaurant, and thank you to your wonderful staff for such a great meal." Annie clapped.

The entire table clapped along with her.

"We have a lot to be thankful for. It would take too much time for me to go through the entire list, but please know each of you hold a special place in my heart." Annie's eyes began to well up with tears.

"I think back to earlier years. They were pretty sad and hard to get through. Losing your parents is never easy. I thank God every day I had Grandmother and Auntie and Mary. Mary would be here tonight, but she and Danny are babysitting, and she's getting really good at it, too."

The table laughed.

"I'm thankful to my college sisters, who gave me the idea to start Sweet Indulgence." She nodded to them each separately, blowing them kisses. "I'm very thankful for Jack, who entered the bakery that day to pick up cupcakes for Crystal." She focused on his eyes and smiled. More *oohs* and *ahhs* came. "And, I'm most thankful for the dedicated and very loyal staff, who have made it possible for me to become more of a silent owner." Annie's eyes rested on Peter, Betsy, Toby, and Keith and Morgan who had come into town to visit family during the holidays. "And, Rebecca, ...

where are you?" Annie searched the room for her friend.

Rebecca came forward from behind and waved.

"Thank you, Rebecca, for being a model employee, and for hosting us tonight."

The group turned and applauded Rebecca.

"So, here's to finding your happiness. I've certainly found mine. Merry Christmas!" Annie raised her water glass.

Everyone slid their chairs back and raised their glasses. "Merry Christmas," everyone shouted.

Annie, Jack, Vicky, and Scott stayed behind after everyone had left the restaurant. Annie wanted to express her gratitude to Rebecca and her grandmother once more.

Annie handed Rebecca an envelope. "Merry Christmas, Rebecca. Thanks again for hosting us. It was so good."

"Anytime, I'm grateful for you, too, you know."

Annie cocked her head. "How so?"

"If you hadn't taken a chance on me that day, I might not be where I'm at."

"Oh, please. You already had the skill. You just needed more confidence. And boy, did that ever flourish after only a little time." Annie patted her on the shoulder.

Rebecca walked the couples out the door, and then turned the open sign to closed. She waved to them before turning out the lights.

Vicky and Scott walked with their arms around each other, and Jack and Annie did the same. The brisk night air caused Annie to squeeze her jacket together and they picked up their pace a bit, reaching their cars in a few minutes.

"Thanks for hanging out with us," Annie said to Vicky, the light wind now picking up some and causing her to shudder.

"You better get home and rest. They say rest is the best for pregnant moms."

Annie's eyes widened. "How'd you know?"

"You didn't drink alcohol. You haven't drank any wine or anything for the last few times we've been together. I told you the day I saw you drink water for a toast, then I'd know. So, am I right?" Vicky dug her hands into her pockets of her sweater jacket and shrugged her shoulders.

Annie took her hand out of her pocket and reached for Jack's hand. He laced his fingers with hers. They both nodded at the same time.

Vicky pulled her hands out of her pockets and rushed toward them, dancing around them as she hugged them tightly. "I'm so happy for you two!"

"We were waiting until we could tell Jack's folks and Grandmother and Auntie. They come over Christmas Eve."

"Does Mary know?"

Annie smirked. "I swear, that girl knew before I did."

"She has that uncanny skill, right?" Vicky laughed.

"We have some good news, too." Scott said, stepping in close to them all. Vicky urged him to tell by nodding. "We are adopting another child, a little boy from Korea."

"Oh, guys, that's so wonderful! Jasmine will have a sister." Annie's eyes welled. "Sorry—hormones," she said, wiping the tears away.

"Ashton will be a big brother, and Jasmine will be a big sister," Vicky said, crying now, too.

"And they'll be the best of friends. Because, there's nothing sweeter than sharing iced tea, backyard barbecues, and bonfires with good friends. Everything is sweeter in Carolina."

"Everything is sweeter in Carolina," they echoed as they clasped hands and looked up to the brightly shining stars overhead.

CHAPTER TWENTY-TWO

After the Christmas Eve dinner, consisting of mostly heavy appetizers, the family settled into various comfy chairs, sofas, and even the floor. A few remained seated at the dining room table. The house didn't seem quite so large when everyone came over.

Crystal and Ashton played tag, running all through the house, laughing with the two dogs on their butts. Grandmother and Auntie were in deep discussion with Jack's grandparents. The only people who seemed to be a bit bored were Susan and Preston Powell, Danny's folks. Annie sighed as she watched Mary trying her hardest to be the thoughtful daughter-in-law and engage them in conversation. Annie wanted to go over and gently smack Susan on the shoulder and tell her to lighten up, but it wouldn't do any good.

Jack started the fire and sat down on the hearth. His eyes rested on Annie's, giving her a nod it was time.

She smiled back at him, letting him know she understood. She beckoned him to join her by curling her index finger toward him. "Everyone, I have an announcement." She laced her arm with Jack's.

Grandmother tapped her cane a few times to get everyone to stop talking. "Annie has a special announcement to make." Lilly screwed up her face as she locked eyes with Annie. "Please, child, hurry up and tell us what we already know."

Annie widened her eyes and then shot Mary a look, letting her know that she had something coming to her for letting out the secret. Mary shook her head and mouthed, "*I didn't say anything.*"

Annie knitted her brows. "Tell you what you already know? What is it that everyone knows before I tell them, Grandmother?" Annie decided to play along to get Grandmother's goat.

Grandmother cleared her throat. "You've been really tired lately. You cry at the drop of a hat, and let's see, I think you've gained a few pounds." Her eyes settled on Annie's belly.

Annie straightened her posture. "Grandmother Lilly, nothing can get by you, can it?"

"Nope, and don't even try. When's the baby due?"

"Baby!" Milly said, jumping up and almost dumping poor Ashton to the ground.

"Dear Lord, Milly, where've you been?" Grandmother furrowed her brows.

"I didn't catch it, but now I get it. You're having another baby." Milly ran over to Jack and hugged him, then made her way to Annie.

After the commotion of the announcement drifted back to normalcy, everyone started handing out suggestions for baby names. Grandmother Cora felt her mother's name would be suitable if it was a girl, and Polly offered a male version of Robert—Roberta.

Milly held her hand up in protest. "Nope, I got it. Jacanna."

The entire group at once yelled, "Jacanna?"

Milly heaved her shoulders up and down. "You know. Jac ... anna," she said enunciating each syllable, to clearly show it was part of Jack's and Annie's names.

Grandmother didn't hold back. "That's the most ridiculous name I've ever heard. They are most certainly not going to name her that."

Annie bit down on her lip. Things were beginning to heat up.

Jack wrapped his arm around Annie, pulling her close. "Should we let them know we already picked out a name?"

"No."

Jack pursed his lips. "I thought we settled on Carolina?" he whispered.

Annie's eyes twinkled as she lovingly smiled at him. "We did, but if we tell them the name, then they'll know we're having a girl. And I want to wrap this Christmas Eve celebration up." Annie cracked a smile, while playfully nudging him.

Jack tossed his head back and roared with laughter. "I see you've met my family, huh?" He leaned in and kissed her. "I love you, Mrs. Powell."

"Love you more," she said, holding him with one arm, while resting her other hand on her belly. "And, just so you know, I adore your family."

Jack's eyes moved from one set of couples to another as he watched them decipher the news. It was traveling through the crowd like wild fire. "We have a great family. They're not perfect, but when the chips are down, they come out in full force. That's what families do."

Annie nodded. "I'm so thankful to have them all in Ashton's and soon, Carolina's life."

"Oh, look, Grandmother is calling for me. I think

they're ready to go home." Jack pulled away from Annie and headed over to both Lilly and Patty.

SNUGGLED IN THE CRUX OF HIS ARM, ANNIE CLOSED HER eyes and listened to the sounds the dark house made at night—the occasional thumping of ice being made in the freezer, the humming of the heater as it began to wind up. She could hear the trees softly swaying in the December night breeze, along with an occasional hoot from a nearby owl. And if she listened really hard, she could hear sounds of little marsh birds and insects, which seemed to be the most vocal at night. And soon, with the contentment of being in the arms of the man she loved, Annie drifted off to sleep.

AFTERWORD

A NOTE FROM THE AUTHOR

I hope you enjoyed the third and final installment of the Charleston Harbor Novels. So many readers have expressed their love for Annie and Jack and their quirky families. If you enjoyed reading them, please take a moment and leave a review from whichever retailer you purchased the book from. Thanks again for taking the time and spending your money on purchasing one of my books. With so many to choose from, I'm honored you chose mine.

ABOUT THE AUTHOR

Debbie currently lives in northern California with her husband and two rescue dachshunds, Dash and Briar.

When Debbie isn't writing or traveling to a book signing, she's visiting her family on the east coast, or traveling to other places on her bucket list. She enjoys hiking with her husband and riding on the back of their motorcycle.

An avid animal lover, Debbie donates a portion of her proceeds to animal rescue organizations. When you purchase one of her books, you're also helping a furry pet with shelter, food, and ultimately a new home!

She loves to hear from fans. Here's how to connect with her.

Sign up for her newsletter and receive a free gift for joining!

Website: https://www.authordebbiewhite.com

facebook.com/debbiewhitebooks

twitter.com/dwhiteauthor

instagram.com/caliromanceauthor

pinterest.com/authordwhite

90375604R00137

Made in the USA
San Bernardino, CA
09 October 2018